Us Against Everybody: A Detroit Love Tale

A Novel By
Miss Candice

Text LEOSULLIVAN to 22828 to join our
mailing list!

To submit a manuscript for our review, email
us at leosullivanpresents@gmail.com

Acknowledgements

As always, I thank God for giving me the gift of writing, and the strength to carry on. Without him, none of this is possible. ♡

I can't believe this is book number 8! Sometimes I still can't believe I'm a published author. This has been my dream for years! Since I was in the seventh grade. The feeling is so surreal. I thank my publisher, Leo Sullivan, for giving me this platform to share my writing with others. Also, big thanks to Tamra. Leo couldn't have hired a better assistant for LSP. You are the absolute best!

As usual, I thank my readers! I absolutely love and appreciate the support from each and every one of you! I hope you fall in love with Vice like you did with Keem. I've gotta say... I sure did! Vice is bae! LOL.

I'm going to keep this short and simple because I find myself saying the same thing in each and every one of the acknowledgments of my books. LOL. Anyway, I hope you all enjoy this first installment to my new series. As always, I've given it my all! Don't forget to leave a review – good or bad – once you finish!

Thank you!

Synopsis

Love is a funny thing. Without notice, it creeps up on you and takes over every rational decision you make. Without thought, you're willing to do whatever necessary to be with the one who's stolen your heart. Even if that means risking your life, and being cut off from family in the process. And for Vice, that was a loss Storm was willing to take.

After giving up on finding true love, the handsome and captivating, Vice crosses the threshold of Storm's heart. As destiny would have it, the couple contributes glee and cherishing moments to each other lives –putting an end to the doubts surrounding their union.

Nonetheless, naysayers and skeptics couldn't be more furious of the doting couple. While the two are building one another up, their enemies are plotting to tear them down. Death, disloyalty, and animosity fuels the schemes against Storm and Vice, but the two aren't going down without a fight.

Sneak Peek.

Twenty minutes later we were down town Detroit, on our way to Starters. There wasn't a parking space, so we walked hand in hand the small distance to the restaurant. For this nigga to only hustle over by seven mile, people sure knew him everywhere we went. I swear everybody we passed spoke to him. I almost had to whoop some ass too.

We were almost to the restaurant when we were getting ready to pass a group of females – excuse me, I mean hood rat, thot ass bitches! As soon as they seen Vice they hurried over to us.

"Hey *stranger*," said one of the bitches eyeing me up and down.

Vice glanced at her and said, "Wassup."

One of her friends chimed in, "What's been up with you nigga? Why haven't you hit my girl up?"

I'm assuming her 'girl' is the tacky bum bitch that called him stranger. Vice didn't say anything to her. He pulled me closer and we kept walking while these bitches walked with us.

"Damn KiKi, I guess he wifed up now," said another one of her friends while giggling.

"I guess so huh," said KiKi, "It ain't shit he'll be done with this bitch in a couple weeks and calling me. Ain't that right Vice?"

Vice stopped. I mean he stopped dead in his tracks, with no warning. I wasn't really fazed by the jealous bitches. As long as neither of them stupidly put hands on me I was good. All that tough, slick talking was just that. Talking. But Vice was visibly annoyed and he let them know it.

He turned to me and said, "I apologize lil' mama." I started to ask why but he turned to KiKi and her entourage and said, "Get the fuck on. Dirtball ass bitches. I didn't call her because I was done with her." He frowned up and said, "Stop disrespecting before I make y'all ignorant ho's regret even stepping to me."

KiKi's friend started to say something but she intervened, "Let's just go. If basic is what he likes then ay!"

"Far from basic sweetie," I smiled.

Vice turned my way and shook his head, "Don't ever, I mean ever, waste your breath on jealous females who aren't even a tad bit close to your level."

And then we walked away.

I couldn't even trip. Like I've said so many times, Vice is a very handsome dude. I won't be naïve and think I'm the only woman he's been with. Bitter bitches is expected while dealing with a man of his stature. Vice is the type of man any woman would want to hold on to. Look at the lengths Joslyn went. Hell, I just met him not even two months ago and I don't want to lose him. So I can't act an ass when bitches step out of boundary. I won't give them the satisfaction of my anger. I'll simply smile just like I did before. It's nothing. I don't see any women as competition. Why should I? When I will do whatever necessary to keep this man happy.

Before we walked into Starter's, Vice stopped and turned to face me.

"You aight brown skin?"

"Yeah, I'm good. Why wouldn't I be?"

He nodded, "I hope you understand my apology. I can be a nutty nigga some times and I'd rather you not see that side of me."

I smiled, "I like all sides of you, Vice. It's cool."

"It's not. I don't want you getting any bad ideas about fucking with a nigga. I can only control myself; I can't control what comes out of the mouths of past broads. I can only try and hope that you peep the

9

serenity in my voice when I say you're the only one I see."

I just kissed him, grabbed his hand and walked into the bar.

I texted my daddy to let him know we were here, while Vice was conversing with a group of men. He held me close to him the entire time. I smiled sweetly as he introduced me as his wifey. It felt good to be introduced as such but one of the men made me feel uncomfortable. He kept staring at me and shit. I had to excuse myself to get away from him. Vice didn't give me their names so I didn't know who the fuck he was. Even if he did tell me their names I still wouldn't know who the guy was. He was bold as fuck for staring at me like my nigga ain't nutty as hell.

On my way to the restroom I bumped into my daddy. He gave me a hug and immediately asked me where my 'new boyfriend' was. Daddy was being casual but I knew he wanted to grill him. That's what he always did when I started a new relationship. He didn't like my ex and I should've took that as a sign right then and there. But I just figured he was hating like daddy's do. I prayed like fuck he liked Vice because I was going to be with him regardless.

"You look gorgeous as usual, Stormy," said my daddy hugging me again.

I smiled, "and you look like you're on a hunt for thotties."

I was telling the truth. Although my daddy was damn near fifty he didn't look a day over thirty five. Mack was handsome, and dressed in nothing but designer clothing. He kept up with the trends and even had a head full of long neat dreadlocks. He's deep brown skin with thick eyebrows and dark brown doe shaped eyes with long eyelashes. Let's not get on his body. My daddy swore up and down he was a young cat. He wore a goatee and I was happy he didn't give in to the 'bearded' trend. When we went out together people thought we were a couple. Ugh.

"You know me, baby girl," said my daddy with a smile and wink. "Now where he at?"

I pointed across the room, "Right there."

Immediately, he tensed up, "You fucking with Vice?"

"Fucking with?" I frowned, "What's wrong with you? He's my boy—

"Ex-boyfriend," said my daddy retrieving his phone from the back pocket of his True Religion jeans, "End that."

I looked at him like he was crazy, "What? Daddy no. I'm a grown wom—

"A grown woman but still my daughter. I said end that shit Storm," he yelled drawing attention to us.

I looked across the room hoping Vice didn't see what was going on and he did. I prayed to God he didn't come over here, but yeap, he did. I'd liked to run out of there when he walked up to us and extended his hand to my daddy with a smirk. It was obvious that the two of them knew each other and weren't too fond. I just didn't understand it. How could they have beef with each other and they were from two different eras?

"Wassup, pops?" said Vice.

My daddy looked him and up down, ignoring his extended hand. He looked to me and said, "Get rid of this joker, Storm." And then he walked away.

"What was all of that about," I asked with an attitude.

Vice laughed and bit on his bottom lip, "That's pops huh?"

"Yeah, now what the fuck is going on?"

"Dear ol' dad don't like me, brown skin," he said before grabbing my hand, "Let's get the fuck out of here ma."

I yanked away, "Nah, obviously some real shit is going on. I need to know why he don't like you, Vice!"

He stared at me long, and hard before replying, "I'd rather not talk about it here."

Just as I was opening my mouth to say something my daddy and two other big burly guys approached us. They told Vice he had to leave. I was stuck. I didn't know who to go with. My loyalty lies with my daddy because he's my daddy. But damn, I'm feeling Vice and I feel like something is definitely wrong. I was confused.

Vice though, he was unbothered.

He smiled and winked at me, "I'll hit you up later, lil' mama. Don't worry 'bout none of this."

My daddy stood in front of me and said to Vice, "Get yo young reckless ass up outta here boy. You won't be hitting her up." Then he turned to me, "Aight that right, princess?"

I just shook my head and watched them escort Vice out of the bar. I walked off in the direction of my daddy's office. Just as expected he was following behind me. When we made it to his office, he slammed the door shut.

"Do you know what type of nigga you dealing with, Storm," he yelled in my face.

I was caught off guard. My daddy never yelled at me. He always treated me like his princess. In his eyes I could do no wrong. I was hurt so like a big baby, I cried.

"What?! What is the fucking problem?"

He pointed his finger in my face, then walked around his desk and took a seat, "You gone watch your mouth, for one Storm. You might be grown but let's not forget who the parent is here." He slammed his fist down on his cherry oak desk, "Damn! How long you been fucking with that boy?"

"What is the problem daddy!? Seriously."

He rubbed his goatee, "Vice killed Lando."

I wanted to say 'tell me something I don't already know' but I just stood there with my arms crossed over my chest. Lando wasn't anything to us for real. I mean, sure we grew up in the same hood and what not but it's not like we considered him family. He wasn't to us what Jai is. So I really can't understand the problem.

"Okay, what's that got to do with us?"

My daddy chewed on his bottom lip and shook his head, "Don't say one word to your mama..."

"About what?"

"Lando and them other niggas worked for me. I was his connect."

[CHAPTER ONE]
VICE

I sat behind the wheel of my 'Lac, peeping the scenery. Kids played on the playscape and swung on the swing set. I retrieved my Galaxy 6 from the cup holder and called my right hand man, Reek. He answered on the first ring.

"Wassup, brodie?"

"Postpone it. Kids all around this bitch," I replied with a headshake.

"You sure? I got the scope locked on the weak nigga right now."

"That bitch accurate," I paused, "Dude out here with his seeds."

I felt a little eerie about murdering a man in front of his kids. No matter how much hate and animosity I had for Orlando, I didn't want to kill him like that. It was more about the emotional damage it would do to his children than anything. I could give less than a fuck about him dying. His time had come. It was that man's time to go. But not now. I couldn't order a hit out on him like this.

"Yeah it's accurate, bro. What's the word?"

I started my engine, "Wait on it. Keep them young niggas on his tail though. We'll take care of him later on tonight."

Reek cursed, "Fuck. I was ready to put an end to his ass, Vice," he paused, "But aight, we can hold off on it."

I ended the call, then pulled off and headed in the direction of home, watching Lando smile and push his son on the swing in the rearview. Homeboy didn't know how close he'd come to death. He stood there smiling without a care in the world. He knew I was after him, but you wouldn't be able to tell by the look on his face. He had a smile only a father would know about. I wasn't a father, but his joy was obvious. His kids were happy too. They wore the same carefree smile. I couldn't take that smile away from them. I couldn't let them witness their father's brains being splattered all over the playground. I couldn't torture them like that, so I rescheduled the hit. He was dying. Just not now.

I live in Detroit, Michigan where the motto is to *either kill or be killed.* I'm a kill type of man. I prey on niggas before they can even scheme up a plan good enough to get me. You have to possess that type of state of mind in the business I'm in–the drug business, that is. I've been going on and on and I haven't introduced myself; I'm Vice. My mother must've felt creative in the delivery room. Vice is my government name, and I don't go by anything other than it. I figured it was a small token of respect to pay my late mother.

Becoming a drug dealer wasn't something I wanted. I'm twenty-two years old and I've been in this business for about four years. I was forced to become a part of the statistics. As a kid, I dreamt of being a doctor, but those plans came to a halt after my mother passed away. I figured Pops divorced me too once he left her. I hadn't seen my father since before he divorced my mother, so I was forced to take care of myself. It had been over ten years since I saw his weak ass. I didn't know a thing about drugs, but I learned quickly. Old head by the name of Rico put me on. That man taught me everything I knew. Dog gave me my first rock to sell. He was more of a father to me than my actual pops ever was.

After my mom's passed away, I moved with my auntie and my cousins, over on Riopelle off Seven Mile. I was only seventeen at the time, but my cousins and I were heavy weed smokers. One cold ass winter day, I was sitting outside in the back of the house firing up yet another bammer ass reggies blunt, when our neighbor Rico walked up on me. Immediately, I put the blunt out. Dude was an old head and I didn't need him running off to snitch on me.

"It's cool, young blood. I want to holler at you about something real quick," he said as he took a seat next to me.

I started to fire the blunt back up, but he stopped me.

"Don't bother sparking that dirt ass weed back up," said Rico, reaching in the pocket of his Al Wissam leather, "Try this."

I took the blunt from him and lit it. Off rip, I knew it wasn't the shit that was floating around the hood. I asked him where he got it from, and he tossed a crack rock in my lap. I looked at it, not knowing what the fuck it was. When I asked him what it was, he laughed and told me it was my way to the top. Rico told me he came across some drugs while he was out of state. He told me he saw something in me he didn't see in my cousins, or any of the other young niggas in the hood. Unlike them, I stayed in school and stayed out the way of bullshit. He told me he was too old to get back in the game and wanted me to sell it. At first I laughed at him, and told him to get the fuck on. I told him that for weeks until I found myself homeless, staying at the shelter because auntie Kesh ended up getting evicted.

I hopped on that Woodward bus, heading to the Seven Mile bus quick as fuck after staying up in the Detroit Rescue Mission shelter for two nights. Rico was happy to see me, and I was happy he hadn't given the drugs to anyone else. I thought he wanted me to sell for him, but he told me it was mine, and that he wanted me to make my own bread. To this day, I look out for blood because that was some real ass shit. He

19

was the only person back then to actually give a damn about me.

I haven't always been on top of the drug game though. Back in the day, some cat by the name of Keem ran shit. At the time I was a little nigga, but I heard shit about how my mans ran the city with an iron fist. Like I said before, I didn't intentionally get involved in this lifestyle. The shit kind of just fell in my lap. Like, literally.

Shit slowed down after Keem and his squad disappeared. It was a drought on all the good weed. I mean, a nigga couldn't cop a good bag of green for shit! Not only that, but the fiends were dropping like flies. The shit on the streets after they left was straight up garbage. Everything changed once Rico put me on though.

I stopped at a red light on Seven Mile and Van Dyke, and watched a sexy brown skin walk across the street. She looked to be five feet; a little shorter than what I liked but, her looks were model-like. I watched her walk into the liquor store. The light turned green, and I made a quick left and parked in the store's parking lot. I shut the engine off and hopped out. I wouldn't normally do this, but it was something about brown skin's sex appeal that had me drawn. Her beauty was like one I hadn't witnessed in this hood.

When I walked in the store, the first voice I heard was a rat named Jai. No matter what hood I was in, she was always there. Sometimes I thought the broad was stalking me.

I walked right by her and she yelled, "Hey Vice! You can't speak, nigga?"

I looked at her. Jai was very attractive. She had golden skin that matched her curly golden hair. She had a nice body as well, but she didn't know how to carry herself like a woman. There she was standing in the liquor store dressed in booty shorts and a halter top. Jai stayed fly though; it was just that she dressed like the whore she was known as.

"Sup, Jai?"

She eyed me up and down, "You."

I kept walking. Jai always threw the pussy at me, but I never gave her the time of day. She was a gold digger with pride; so much pride that she had the words tatted on her wrist. I wasn't the richest nigga out, but I had a nice amount of money. She knew that. Hell, everybody in the hood knew that. I knew she had motives, so I never paid her any mind.

I searched the store for sexy brown skin and found her looking in the freezer, struggling to reach a Pepsi on the top shelf. I stood there watching her for a second. She was oblivious to my presence. Shorty climbed on the first shelf and reached up, still unable

21

to reach the pop. She hopped down and sucked her teeth.

"Are you going to just stand there watching or are you going to help me?" asked brown skin without even looking my way. I thought she hadn't noticed me, but she did, in fact.

I walked over to her, "I thought you had it, shorty. You climbing on shelves and shit."

She stood to the side with her mouth twisted up, "Yeah, well I had a man who appears to be about six feet watching and not helping."

I reached up and grabbed the pop, then handed it to her. She thanked me and then walked away. I followed her and started to ask for her name, but once she addressed Jai as sis, I walked out of the store. Birds of a feather flock together. Whoever shorty was, she was only out for a quick buck like her 'sis'. I never associated myself with those types. The women I spent time with worked for what they had. They weren't out here looking for a handout. Shit, I should've known she was a rat; she was in one of the grimiest hoods in the D.

I hopped behind the wheel of my 'Lac and watched them walk out of the store. Although she was with Jai, she didn't possess the same kind of outspoken hood rat ways as Jai. She walked with her 'sis' with an uneasy smile on her face, while Jai yelled at a group of niggas sitting outside of the store. One of the guys approached brown skin, and it looked like she politely rejected him. My stereo was a little loud and my windows were rolled up, so I lowered them both.

"No, I don't have a man. I'm simply not interested," said brown skin.

"Ay Jai, who is this uppity bitch you got running with you?" asked ol' boy.

Jai opened her big ass mouth as usual. I didn't understand why this broad thought she could talk to men any kind of way. Jai could indeed scrap, but she often tried that shit with niggas–and she got away with it. Eventually she was going to come across the wrong nigga and he was going to pop her in that big ass mouth of hers.

"What? Nigga you better calm that shit down! Don't call my sister a bitch! You mad cause she's not interested in your dirty ass?" Jai stood in his face, "Get the fuck on, bum ass!"

I chuckled. This bitch really thought she had real nigga balls. I sat there watching. Brown skin stood back shaking her head. I admired the way she carried herself. Her full lips were drawn in her mouth, and her hands were in the back pocket of her stonewash-destroyed jean shorts.

"Bitch. Fuck you and yo ugly ass friend. Shit, I was trying to get some head up out her," replied ol' boy.

Brown skin grabbed Jai's arm, "Come on sis, let's just go."

Jai yanked away, "you gon' let this nigga disrespect you like that?"

Ol' boy stepped in between Brown skin and Jai, shoving brown skin in the process. I watched as his weak ass niggas sat back and watched everything transpire. Just like some bum niggas to let home boy act an ass like that. My niggas knew better than to be involved in some petty shit like that. Ol boy was salty as hell about brown skin rejecting him. Weak niggas couldn't take rejection. He should've known brown skin was way out of his league. One look at brown skin and you'd know you had to be an up to par type of nigga to push up on her. He wore a dingy durag, oversized played Girbaud jean shorts, busted forces, and a wife-beater that was just as dingy as his durag.

"Excuse you," yelled brown skin.

Ol boy turned his attention to brown skin and in one swift move, he had his hands around her neck. I had seen enough.

I hopped out of the whip and slammed the door. Heads turned towards me, and his weak ass niggas yelled, "What up Vice, bro!" with their hands extended. I walked straight past all of their weak asses. Ol boy noticed me coming his way and let go of her.

"Damn Vice, this one of yo bitches," asked dingy. "My bad bro, I wasn't trying to step on yo toes!"

I ignored him and pushed him away from brown skin. Jai was hysterical, and I told her to calm her ass down and go home. Brown skin looked up at me with nervous eyes. Obviously she wasn't from this hood. I asked her if she was alright, and she nodded her head. Jai was still trying to fight.

I grabbed her arm, "Ay, calm that shit down, Jai. Take yo friend away from up here."

She shot another threat at ol boy before she grabbed brown skin's hand and walked away. Brown skin looked over her shoulder as they walked away, and I nodded at her. She winked at me and gave me a smile.

"Fuck you up here clowning for, lil nigga," I asked ol boy.

"Bitches was disrespecting," he coolly replied.

I decided not to say anything about peeping the whole ordeal. I walked away while they asked stupid questions about being put on. I would never put those type of dudes on. They were stupid and immature.

They'd only be a problem for me, and I had enough of those as is.

I hopped back in the whip and sped off, blasting Drake's new ten bands. If you haven't noticed, I'm a different type of dude. If I see some shit popping off that I don't like, I normally interfere, especially if it involves a woman – cute or ugly. As you see, I'm well respected in the hood. I'm not the most paid, most made nigga out here, but I have a few hoods of my own. I run shit from Seven Mile to the Six. I supply the majority of the dope traps over here, so as I said, niggas look up and respect me. I don't have to act a complete ass to get my point across neither.

I sped down Seven Mile with my windows rolled down, enjoying the summer breeze. The hood rats were out, and niggas were stunting on every corner. Summertime was my all-time favorite season. The most shit popped off in the summertime. I loved the many festivities and ratchetness that popped off in the hood. The summertime in Detroit was always the crunkest. From cruising Belle Isle to posting up downtown and the numerous drag races; shit stayed popping off.

My phone rung and I looked over at it. Joslyn's pretty yellow face smiled back at me. I turned the radio down and answered, "Wassup lil' mama?"

"Vice, I missed my period."

[CHAPTER TWO]
STORM

"Who was that dude?" I curiously asked my best friend Jai.

"Girl that's Vice's fine ass," replied Jai with a mouthful of pickle and Hot Flaming Cheetos.

We were chilling on her front porch, eating junk food and talking shit as usual. I couldn't keep my mind off the chestnut-colored, thin, almond shaped hazel-brown eyed dude who basically saved us earlier. He was so...different. The way that boy tensed up and fell back was enough confirmation. Whoever the sexy beast of a man was, he wasn't a force to be reckoned with. His stance, his stride...the way he spoke with so much assertiveness...you couldn't help but give him the attention and respect his aura demanded.

I was spending the weekend with my best bitch in the whole wide world. I'm an only child, so I really considered her my sister. Jai could be a little over the top, but I loved her nonetheless. She kept excitement in my boring life. She and I were like night and day, but we've been inseparable since elementary, which was over fifteen years ago.

I was born and raised on the east side of Detroit, over on McNichol's and Davison. I met Jai in the kindergarten, and we've been close ever since.

"I'm not surprised he stepped up and said something. Vice is stand up like that," said Jai, nodding her head while looking down at her Galaxy 6 Edge.

"I am. I've never seen anything like that. Dude fell the fuck back as soon as Vice stepped up," I replied.

Jai looked up at me with a confused frown, "Because, bitch, Vice is a boss over here. That bum ass nigga would've got the piss smacked out of him if he didn't fall back," Jai licked her lips, "That nigga is a mothafuckin boss."

Jai was clearly feeling him, so I figured he was off limits to me. I wondered if she fucked him. I could tell she hadn't though. She would've described him totally different if she had. Jai liked bragging on the niggas she fucked, especially if they looked as good as Vice. He had shown a little interest in the store, but for some reason he didn't try to get on. Maybe he did fuck Jai.

"You fucked him, ho?" I boldly asked with a giggle.

"Nah, girl I wish." She sucked her teeth, "Vice don't be stunting me. But I saw how he was looking at you. Fuck with him girl. That nigga is a hood celebrity; the money and dick run long."

I cracked up laughing. I swear, Jai had no filter.

"Bitch you stupid!"

I was glad she hadn't fucked with him. I'm the type of female that wouldn't touch a nigga with a ten-foot pole if my girl was feeling him, and she was the same way. Jai might've been a little shiesty and a proud gold digger, but she would never step on my toes. We were loyal to one another.

"Speaking of long money, remember Percy's old ass promised me a pink Benz?" I nodded and she continued, "Lying ass nigga! He claim he at the dealership now. But I don't think his ass tryna dish out that type of money."

I laughed, "Shut yo greedy ass up Jai, damn! How much money he don' spent on you? A couple thou? Chill out. I wish I had a nigga spending that type of bread on me."

I could really appreciate that, but I was cool with my little job at Somerset, working at Neiman Marcus. Not to mention, my daddy occasionally threw me ridiculous amounts of money. I was spoiled rotten and always would be. I'm twenty years old, and my father still pays my rent and car note.

"Well you better be willing to throw that ass in a circle for Vice's fine hood rich ass," Jai laughed and showed me her phone, "Peep. I get what the fuck I want!"

I stared at the phone in disbelief. Percy sent her a picture of a pink Benz and a receipt. I couldn't believe men were openly spending money on her like that. He was an old head, so I understood his angle – he was Jai's sugar daddy. Young guys were even spending loads of money on her.

"Spoiled ass, "I replied with a head shake. "Wassup for the day? I don't want to stay posted in the hood all day. Let's go downtown."

Jai nodded and said, "Alright, after his old ass drop my car off we can go."

Three hours later, we were cruising downtown Detroit in Jai's new flamboyant Pink Benz. Beyoncé's Flawless remix spilled out of the car windows as the wind blew through my twenty-two inches of Brazilian hair. I felt good. I was sipping on Avion and Pineapple juice, as was Jai, although she was driving.

The hustle and bustle of Downtown always excited me. Although I was a little reserved and stayed to myself all of the time, I could appreciate the crowdedness of the city. Everyone was out enjoying themselves. Niggas cruised in their old school Chevys with big ass rims, and hood rats walked the strip. Jai found a good spot near Hart Plaza and turned the engine off, leaving the music blasting as we touched our MAC lip gloss up.

"Shit girl, I hope I find me a baller out here tonight. Rent is due in a couple of days and I am not trying to go in my stash," said Jai, looking in the mirror and pressing her powder pink lips together as she rubbed her lip gloss in.

I brushed my bone straight weave. "I'm sure you will. Hopefully somebody catches my eye. He ain't gotta be the richest, but ya girl is lonely."

And that I was. I hadn't been in a committed relationship since I was eighteen, and that lasted a little over a year. Nico ended up getting one of his side bitches pregnant, and I had enough. I put up with a lot of bullshit dealing with him, from hood rats in my inbox to altercations and a few fists fights. I fought for that nigga, but when Tiffney sent me pictures of the two of them at an ultrasound appointment I was done! D-O-N-E. It took me a minute to get my emotions in order, but after a month of sulking, I was good–good, but single and horny.

"I know you are, boo!" Jai closed the sun visor, "we gon' find you a man tonight, bitch!"

I looked at Jai like she was crazy. When she said *we* were going to find me a man, she meant it. Jai would walk around Hart Plaza literally searching for niggas, and even talking for me. I didn't need that type of attention, so I told her ass to fall back.

After we were done making sure our pretty was on fleek, we hopped out of the car. We were two of the baddest females walking around Downtown. You couldn't tell us shit. We exuded confidence.

"Let's walk the Riverwalk first," suggested Jai.

I nodded in agreement. I was glad I wore Jordan's and not any cute little heels or uncomfortable ass flats. I rarely dressed up anyway. I wore destroyed shorts, a pair of Jordan thirteens, and a white crop top. My twenty-two inches of Brazilian hair was bone-straight, touching the small of my back. My mama had just arched and filled in my brows, and put my individual lashes on. Jai was dressed pretty much the same, which was dressed down for her. Still, she was cute with her blonde twenty-four inches of Malaysian and her golden sun-kissed skin.

As soon as we stepped foot on the walkway, niggas was watching. Unlike me, a lot of niggas knew who Jai was. They were so busy watching me trying to get a piece of the new meat. I didn't get down like that though. Them niggas didn't want shit but to get the pussy. I was good on that. I didn't talk to dudes who came at me all cocky and rude like. I needed a nigga to respect me, and he had to be nice looking. Because of my standards, dirty niggas thought I was stuck up. I just knew my worth.

We were standing by the railings, looking over at Canada when a group of guys approached us. They had a different type of swag about them, so I played nice. One in particular stood out to me since he couldn't keep his slanted browns off me. He stepped to me and extended his hand. I shook it and he introduced himself as B.

"Nice to meet you, B, I'm Storm."

He rubbed his chin, "That's a dope name, Storm. How you doing today?"

"Thanks, I'm good. How bout yourself?"

"Better now, since I've met this beauty by the name of Storm."

I giggled, "Check you out. You came prepared with the game, huh?"

He laughed, "Not game baby, all real." He took his iPhone from his designer jeans, "Can I call you sometimes?"

"You don't even know if I have a man or not, B. In a rush, are we?"

He licked his full lips, "You right. But check it, if you had a man I don't think you would've continued the conversation. Unless dude a sucker and you want a nigga like me?"

I laughed. He was corny as fuck, but I found it a little cute. He was trying hard as hell, so I told him I didn't have a man and gave him my number. B wouldn't give me his government name just yet. I found it childish, but a lot of niggas in the hood was like that so I didn't sweat him. We were the same age. He was a college dropout who hustled here and there. B was dressed nice, which told me he hustled a lot more than what he claimed. He said he was single, but you're never sure these days with these cheating ass niggas. I wasn't trying to jump into a relationship with him anyway, so it didn't really matter if he was lying or not.

[CHAPTER THREE]
JAI

Ryan was happy as hell to get my phone number. He wore a big stupid grin on his ugly face. I pretended that I was actually feeling his ass. I rubbed on the side of his face that was covered with the most bumps to stroke his ego. Niggas loved that type of shit. I knew he was insecure about them, but I played it off like I didn't even notice! His ass probably was at home staring in the mirror, worried about not pulling any bitches because of them–but baby, I couldn't care less. A nigga could be as ugly as Flava Flav, but if he had bread then I was on his ass.

Ryan was the ugliest out of the group of five, but he was decked out in designer clothing, wore Cartier buffs, on his feet were a pair of high-top Christian Louboutin gym shoes, and his jewels were iced out. One look at him and you could tell he was the wealthiest of the group. That's all I cared about. A broke, cute nigga couldn't do a damn thing for me. Ryan might've been ugly, but his money wasn't. I didn't discriminate when it came to the paper. I had to get paid by any means necessary, and ugly niggas appreciated bad bitches more, so all I seen was dollar signs as I stared into his cocked eyes.

There's power in pussy, and I was taught that if you were good at something to never do it for free; I'm a pro at this sex shit. I never just blatantly threw it out there. You had to earn this pussy. Don't get it twisted;

36

I'm far from a prostitute. I just don't believe in fucking niggas unless I'm getting something out of it. I wish Storm could understand that, but she was a goody goody–a goody goody with no stash, but I love my girl.

Anyway, Ryan kept talking about how sexy I was, so I knew I had him under a spell already! I made plans to hit him up as soon as possible. I needed my rent paid, and I wasn't going in my stash for it. Fuck that, I needed more bundles and some clothes. I'm not irresponsible, but if you can get a sucka to pay your rent, why not take advantage?

I arched my back a little, pushing my 32DDs in his face. He tried his best, but he couldn't keep his eyes off them.

I rubbed his head full of waves and said, "I'm glad I decided to come to the Riverwalk after all."

He licked his black lips, "I'm glad I did too, shawty."

Ryan was from Atlanta. He played linebacker position on the football team here at Michigan State University, where he was studying business. He was only in the D for the weekend, visiting his cousins. He'd be here more often if it was up to me. I had to show him mad attention if I wanted things to work my way.

I've always been spoiled, thanks to my late daddy. He spoiled me rotten and when he passed away, I figured it'd always be a man's responsibility to take care of me. His name was Jay, and he was the only person I had. My mama died during childbirth, so I've never been fortunate enough to have one of those. Daddy did whatever it took to make sure bills were paid, the flyest clothes were on my back, and food was on the table. He didn't sell dope, but he held down three jobs and took damn good care of home. I was devastated when he died two weeks after my twelfth birthday. I was basically forced to take care of myself.

I stayed with Storm and her people for a little while, until my nothing ass auntie figured I was supposed to be with her. What she cared about more than me was the monthly checks she'd get for taking me in. I never saw a dime of that money but hell, it wasn't like I was broke. I've had niggas buying me snacks and little shit here and there since my daddy passed away. I was eating, so I was good.

When I came of age, snacks and petty shit wasn't enough, so I moved on up. Now I had old ass niggas buying me whips, paying my rent, and lacing me with bread. The young fools dished out cash too, but them old wrinkled ball niggas paid the most. I spent up all of their lil' pension money.

I licked my lips and told Ryan I would call him as soon as I got home. I was too. I wasn't lying to his ass. He looked at me like he didn't believe me. Ryan was in pure disbelief period. He wasn't used to a bitch of my stature showing interest. I was five foot five with golden skin, high cheekbones, dimples, and full lips. My eyes were brown and what some considered dreamy. My ass wasn't the fattest, but it was round with a little plump to it. My titties were my best asset next to my face. He probably was used to basic bum bitches, which I was far from. Yeah, I'm feeling myself. Hell, I'm always feeling myself even on my worst days, and I've never even seen one of those!

Storm was finishing up her convo with Ryan's cousin with a big smile on her face. B was cute as hell, but his money wasn't as long as Ryan's. That's where Storm constantly fucked up at. She took looks over the obvious overflow of money Ryan had.

I intertwined my arm in Storm's, and we walked away.

"Home boy corny as hell, but I can fuck with him," said Storm as she saved B's phone number.

"His cousin corny too, but he breaded the fuck up so it's cool," I replied with a laugh.

"I ain't sayin' she a gold digger, but she ain't fuckin with no broke niggas," said Storm, reciting Kanye's lyrics while laughing.

"Yaaas bitch, no broke niggas," I yelled, drawing attention to us.

Us Against Everybody: Miss Candice

[CHAPTER FOUR]
VICE

I sat on the hood of my car watching Joslyn from a distance. She had just told me she missed her period, but her reckless ass was out here drinking liquor and cutting up with her girls. She could've possibly been pregnant, but she didn't care enough to stay her ass at home. I was downtown with my nigga Reek and she had no clue. If Joslyn was indeed pregnant, it wasn't mine. I couldn't understand why she called me with that bullshit when she knew I stayed strapped extra tight when I hit bitches. I won't front though...Joslyn was once my girlfriend of a year and a half, and I used to hit it raw but we've been broken up for over two months, so I made sure jimmy was on extra tight when we slipped up and fucked every now and then.

I watched her smile and flirt with a lame nigga that approached her. Joslyn ain't a hoodrat, but she has hoodrat ways. She often carried herself like a woman and had a job, but it was in settings like this where she'd let loose and cut up. In fact, I met her down here. This was the spot for her and her girls. I shook my head and sipped from my bottle of D'usse.

No longer being with Joslyn was good for me. She was straight, but sometimes too clingy-more now than she was when we were a couple, which was a

41

little crazy. She didn't want anyone else to have me, but she didn't do a good job at keeping me herself.

"Aye bro, ain't that Jos?" asked Reek.

I laughed, "Hell yeah, that's her."

Reek shook his head full of dreads, "Hot as cayenne pepper."

Hot is what she was. She was dressed provocatively, which she knew I hated. The high waisted shorts she wore barely covered her yellow ass checks, and her titties were popping out of the tight V-neck tee she had on. But shit, she wasn't my girl anymore, so it wasn't like I could walk up to her on some trip shit. Besides, she didn't even know I was here. This was probably the way she dressed every time she was out when we were together.

I shook my head and took my eyes off her just to meet the eyes of brown skin. She smiled at me. I nodded at her. It was kind of weird seeing her here. It felt like the shit was meant to be or something. I shook that thought though. Hell, if niggas wasn't at Belle Isle, Chandler, or Rouge, then they were downtown. This was the spot for everybody, so I just took it as what it really was. Everybody posted up here.

"Who the baddie?" asked Reek, taking a pull from his blunt full of Cush.

"Jai's friend. I don't know her yet, but I'm bout ready to change that," I said as I licked my lips and hopped off the hood of the car.

"Shit nigga, you and about twenty other nigga," he laughed, "Betta beat 'em to it bro!"

I laughed and walked in the direction of her. Jai was chopping it up with some guy, while her friend stood there moving her body to the new Future song coming from a car in traffic. She didn't even see me coming. Her eyes were closed, and she was swaying left and right.

I stood behind her and whispered in her ear, "What up?"

She flinched out of surprise. When she turned around to cuss me out, she stopped herself and smiled instead. I had her. She wanted me just as bad as I wanted her. I grabbed her hand and we walked away. Brown skin yelled over her shoulder telling Jai she'd be back. Jai simply smiled, but the woman watching me had a mean mug on her face. I shook my head and rolled my eyes at Joslyn's bad attitude. How she tripping and she was just flirting with a nigga? Females be bugging, I swear.

Joslyn looked like she wanted to come over and start some bullshit. I shot her a mean mug, and she fell back–for the moment, at least. Joslyn really thought I belonged to her, but she knew her place and that I didn't do that drama shit.

Brown skin and I walked across Hart Plaza over to the railings lining the river on the Riverwalk. I stood there staring at her for a few seconds before she shied away and asked me why I was staring at her.

"I'm trying to find a flaw. But shorty, you're flawless," I replied, trying to slick talk her.

Brown skin laughed, "I have flaws Vice, everyone does."

"How is it that you know my name but I don't know yours?"

She smiled and stood face to face with me, then extended her hand, "I'm Storm, Nice to meet you."

"Pleasure to meet you, Storm," I replied before I brought her hand up to my lips and kissed it.

We both laughed and turned our attention to the Princess Boat departing. For the first time in my life, I was a little speechless. I really didn't know how to start up a conversation with her. She was so fuckin' intimidating and like I said, flawless. The women I messed around with were beautiful, but Storm had a regal beauty about her. Shorty was modelesque for sure. She wasn't the thickest, but damn she had a fat ass. Storm had an hourglass figure, and her brown skin was without a blemish. I needed her on my team before anyone else swooped her up–if they hadn't already done so.

"Am I too late?" I asked.

"Too late for what?" inquired Storm with wrinkled eyebrows.

"Too late for you. Are you in a relationship? Please say nah, shorty," I said, giving her puppy dog eyes.

She giggled, "No Vice, you're actually right on time." She took a sip of her drink. "Something has been bugging me though. In the store, you seemed interested and then you didn't. What happened?"

I didn't want to come out and tell her I was cool on her because I thought she was a ho like her friend. I stood there a minute, trying to get my words together so they wouldn't come out disrespectfully.

"Saw you with Jai and thought you weren't my type of woman," I replied as respectfully as possible.

She nodded and put a piece of hair behind her ear, "Mmh, Okay. What changed?" asked Storm, giving me direct eye contact.

I shrugged, "Fuck it. I'm drawn to you. I watched you. The way you move, the way you talk, and how you carry yourself. You're different."

"Watching me? Why?" she asked with a slight frown.

I bit my bottom lip, "Hard not to watch you, Storm. You demand attention baby."

The conversation was going great. She was so down to earth and silly. We stood there at the water kicking it like we didn't just meet minutes ago. She was genuine, and nothing she did was forced on. Most women try so hard to look cute that they sometimes come off stuck up and timid, but nah–not Storm. She let go. Her smile was beautiful. I found myself just staring at her while she laughed at her own jokes. She was so full of life that I wanted to make sure I was always a part of it.

"Vice! Can I talk to you for a minute?!"

I looked over my shoulder at Joslyn, who stood there with a mean mug and her arms folded over her chest. Storm gave me the side-eye and mumbled, "I thought you said you were single, nigga. I don't play side-chick roles."

I laughed and handed her my phone, "I am single, shorty. Put your number in there. Let me go holla at home girl real quick."

When she took the phone away from me, her small fingers brushed up against my big ones. I wanted to grab hold of her and never let her go, but that'd just scare her. I didn't want to come off as intense as I wanted to be, so I played it cool.

I turned away and gave Joslyn a nasty scowl as I approached her. What could this bitch possibly want? She felt some type of way because I was kicking it with Storm. I had just witnessed the slut with another nigga and said nothing. So why sweat me? I calmed myself down because I truly didn't want to disrespect her out here, especially since she could possibly be pregnant.

I stuffed my hands in the back of my designer shorts and tilted my head back a little, "Wassup Jos?"

"Who is she?" she asked with hate dripping from her tongue.

"That's none of your concern," I said, "Wassup Jos?"

She looked past me over at Storm, "Did you just give her your phone?"

I sighed, "Peep, I'm not doing this with you right now. What is it that you want that doesn't concern the pretty little lady standing by the water?"

If looks could kill, I'd be a dead man.

"Excuse me," she yelled.

I walked away. I didn't tolerate drama, and all she was doing was causing a scene. Thankfully, it didn't seem like Storm heard Joslyn's loud mouth. Joslyn didn't deserve further conversation from me. She, like any other woman I've dealt with, knew I didn't do drama. I never wasted my time arguing with an emotional female. I felt like it was a total waste of time. Time is precious, and I'd be a fool to stand there wasting it with ignorance.

I glanced over my shoulder to make sure Joslyn wasn't on my toes. She wasn't. She knew better. My walking away was symbolic for dismissal. I knew I'd receive some emotional ass text messages later. If need be, she'd make the block list.

"My bad, beauty," I said to Storm as I stood behind her, wanting to press my body against hers.

She turned around and leaned her back against the railing, "Why are you standing behind me?"

"Because I wanted to press my body against yours, but I realized it's too soon for such boldness," I honestly replied.

Her eyes nearly popped out of socket in shock, "What?"

I held my hand out for my phone and shrugged, "Just keeping it one hundred with you, baby. Plus, your ass looks damn delicious from this angle."

She handed me my phone, "So what you're saying is that you eat the booty like groceries?"

We both laughed and turned our attention back to the water in front of us. Chilling with her was different. Like I said, shit just flowed perfectly. At times, I found myself at loss of words, but she would always break the silence with a joke or something. I felt a strong connection with her, like no other. The shit actually scared me.

"Vice...ol' girl is marching her ass back over here," said Storm after putting her long ass weave in a ponytail, "Now I don't know what type of shit is going on, but if home girl tries anything, I won't hesitate to smack her ass."

I looked at her and laughed, "You won't have to go Laila Ali out here, lil mama. Shorty ain't stupid enough to say a word to you. Chill out."

I turned away from her and met Joslyn half way. What the fuck was her problem? Broad was trippin on some emotional shit. Like I said, her crazy ass was more possessive over me now than she was when we were together. Looney bitch must've felt some competition. Storm was killing her in every single aspect.

I grabbed Joslyn's arm and pulled her away from Hart Plaza and onto the sidewalk. Her dramatic ass was yelling and trying to pull away from me. What she was doing was trying to stir up attention, but over half of the people out there knew who the fuck I was, and to mind their own business. I mean, all but one save a ho type nigga had the audacity to step to me.

"Ay my man's, leaving the woman alone," he said before grabbing Joslyn's other arm.

I looked at him like he was crazy and kept pulling Joslyn away.

"I said leave her alo—"

I let go of Joslyn, grabbed the gun from my waistband, and touched the middle of his big ass forehead with it, "Fuck out of here, my dude. I'm trying to keep a cool head."

As I warned him, I looked around checking for five-oh. Yeah, they were out there but they paid the small commotion no mind.

He held his short, stubby arms up, "M-my bad man. I'm j-just trying to look out for the girl."

"She's good. But if you don't mind your fucking business, you won't be, my G," I said before concealing my gun back on my waist.

"Vice, it's not even that fucking serious," said Joslyn after the man ran away.

I stuffed my hands in the back pocket of my jeaned shorts, "Fuck you want, Jos? Got damn! A nigga ain't checking for you no more. Get that through your skull! Stop trying to create drama, knowing I don't mess around with it!"

She stood there with her arms folded across her chest. The wind blew her hair in her face, and when she delicately moved it away, I noticed a tear roll down her cheek. Back in the day, when I actually gave a fuck about her, that tear would've did something to me. Now it had no effect. She was only crying because she knew the shit used to bother me. If she knew any better, she would've realized long ago that her crying did nothing now.

"I just told you I might be pregnant and you out here pushing up on new bitches."

I shook my head and smirked, "Jos, my baby, kill it. I just peeped your hot ass talking to a nigga not too long ago. Get the fuck out your feelings, girl." I turned to walk away, "Don't come back over there. If you do, I won't hesitate to make you take your stupid ass home, Joslyn. You can play crazy all you want, but let's not forget who the crazy one really is."

When I made it back over to Storm, lil mama's face was all screwed up.

"What's wrong?"

"Vice... I think you're cool and all, but I don't do drama. Period. So I feel like it's only necessary that I let you know... all I want out of you is friendship."

I took a step back and asked, "How you know that ain't all I want out of you?"

She gave me a twisted-lip look as if to say 'nigga please', and all I could do was laugh.

"Aight lil mama. I feel you. But once you peep that I'm not about games and that I don't do drama neither, you'll want a nigga."

She leaned back on the railing and said, "I want you now. Just not the drama that is currently attached to you."

[CHAPTER FIVE]
STORM

I hadn't heard from Vice in over a week. As much as I'd like to pretend I didn't care, I really did. The nigga must've cut me off because I didn't want to fuck with him. I mean, can you blame me? I just got out of a relationship full of infidelity; why would I want to deal with a nigga who clearly has bitches tripping over him? Nah, nope! I'm sweet on that there.

When I told Jai what happened, she thought I made a stupid decision. Jai might not give a damn and only care about dollar signs, but that's not me. I want to be married with kids one day. I can't see myself settling for a nigga just because of his money and street cred plus, that shit never appealed to me- period. My daddy used to sell dope, and witnessing the stress he put on my mom's was enough for me to be good on those types of niggas. So I was not about to stress over one not calling me.

"Excuse me, can you point me over to the men's department?"

I looked up from my phone and looked into the brown eyes of the girl Vice was arguing with at the Riverwalk. She recognized me too, and turned her nose up at me, but I was professional because I was at work and would rather not get fired for beating the fuck out a bitch.

I smiled, "Right this way." I walked from behind the counter and she followed behind me.

"This is one is my favorite stores to shop for my man at. I've never seen you here. Are you new?"

I looked over my shoulder at her, "Nope, been working here for about two years."

She snickered, "Damn. Two years at a department store? Couldn't be me. How much you making? About nine dollars an hour?"

I wanted to reach back there, grab a fist full of her Marley twist, and get to pounding on her face. The bitch was trying to be funny, talking about *her man*, and taking a crack at my job.

"Oh nah sweetie, a lot more than that," I said with a smile, "Here you are. Let me know if you need anything."

"I just might. Huhh, Vice can be so hard to shop for," she replied while rubbing her stomach, "Father's day is approaching and I want to get him something nice, even though our baby ain't due for a long while."

I just gave the bitch a nod and walked away. Lying ass nigga. Rapped in my ear all night about how he's single with no kids. Huh!

I was standing at my register taking care of a few customers when I heard his voice echoing throughout the store. He was yelling the name Joslyn like he was crazy. My customers looked around the store, trying to find the direction that the voice was coming from, as was I. I didn't want to see his lying ass, but I had to quiet him down before security came through causing an even bigger scene.

I looked over my shoulder and stared into his hazel brown eyes. His eye contact was captivating and full of surprise. Mine was full of anger and disgust.

"Excuse me sir, but I'm going to have to ask the not to yell in the store," I sternly said, as if I didn't know him. Shit, I actually didn't.

He approached my counter and stepped in front if my customer, who shouted, "Hey, wait your turn!"

Vice looked over his shoulder at the small Caucasian woman and said, "Just give me a second, alright?" He turned his attention to me and said, "Why haven't I heard from you?"

"Excuse me, sir, you're holding up my line." I stood on my tiptoes and looked over him, "I believe your *girlfriend* is on her way over." Vice's eye contact was so intense, like he was staring through me and deep within my soul,
"Stop playing with me, lil mama. You and I both know I don't have a girlfriend."

"Vice! Here I am, crazy! I was trying to find you a nice Father's Day gift," she said.

He looked over at her with a frown, "What? Joslyn, go to the car."

She smiled and waved at me on her way out of the store, "It was nice meeting you, girl!"

When she left, Vice started to apologize but I cut his ass clean off, "Sir, I'm going to have to ask you to leave before I resort to calling security." I picked up the phone, "I have a line, and you're holding things up."

He bit down on his teeth, and I noticed his jaw clenching, "Answer your phone in twenty minutes, Storm."

As he walked away I yelled, "Oh, and congratulations on the baby!"

Twenty minutes had turned into an hour, and my stupid ass was still checking my phone. Vice was turning out to be a straight up liar. As much as I wanted to form some type of relationship with him, I knew I couldn't. All a future with him would hold is sadness, and I didn't need that. I needed happiness. We had a strong connection, but things had turned sour as hell.

I scrolled through my contact list until I got down to his name. I didn't want to. Hell, I even struggled to, but I knew it was best for me to just add his ass to the block list, in case he ever did try to call me. Fuck that. His game was way too strong, and I did not want to end up in the situation I was in a while ago. Nah, nope! Not going to happen.

I hovered my thumb over his name, trying my damnedest to press it. In my mind, I kept thinking *'what if I block him as he's calling'*? Then I'd come to my senses and think *'his lying ass said twenty minutes, plus he got a bitch. I do not have time for the drama'*. I was fighting with myself but as usual, the smarts in me kicked in and I made the decision to erase him out of my life. After I did it, I wondered what could have been. I mean shit, I only met him almost two weeks ago, and I couldn't stop thinking about him. Maybe everything that's happened is a sign–a sign to show me to run far away from his sexy brown ass.

I had everything closed up and was on my way home at around ten o'clock. I was dead ass tired, but B hit me up and wanted to go to the bar for a few drinks. I would've told his ass no if Jai and Ryan wasn't meeting us there. Anyway, B's not the most swagged out, bossiest nigga, but at least he's consistent. We talked every day. I found myself forming a small attraction to him, but nothing crazy. I just thought he was a cool ass dude, and someone to occupy my bored time with.

I pulled up at my condo a little after ten fifteen. I stayed in Troy, MI which was a suburban city about twenty minutes outside of downtown Detroit, where we're having drinks. Work had me beat, but I knew I needed to get out and do something. Plus, Jai was all in my ear about how lame I've been. She says all I do is work and sleep. It's true, I cannot argue with that.

Anyway, I took a warm shower and stood in my walk-in closet, trying to decide on what to wear. The June night air was cool and dry. The weather app on my Galaxy 6 told me it was only seventy two degrees out, so I settled with a pair of stonewash jeggings and a sheer, pale pink button-up blouse. I chose a pair of nude flats I copped from H&M not too long ago to wear. Once I was dressed, I filled my eyebrows in, applied some lashes, and put on some eyeliner. On my lips I wore Siss, a nude lipstick by MAC. I decided to wear my hair straight, seeing as though I was too tired to be putting curls in it.

My phone rang just as I was heading out.

Sis.

"I'm on my way, bitch, damn," I answered as I locked my door.

"We've been here for over an hour, hurry yo ass up," Jai shouted.

I knew off rip her ass was drunk as fuck. I rolled my eyes and told her I would be there in thirty minutes. We hung up and shook my head. I already knew what tip she was about to be on, and I really didn't feel like babysitting her ass. Jai is my girl and I loved her like my mama gave birth to her but damn, every time we went out I had to cover her ass. You'll see what I'm talking about soon. Just wait on it.

Thirty minutes later, I was parking at Delux Lounge on Monroe Ave. I hopped out and walked in. The place was packed, and Fetty Wap's My Way was blasting. It didn't take me long to find Jai and them. I just followed her loud laughing. I knew her ass was faded!

I greeted B with a hug, and he told me I smelled good. I smiled and told him he did as well. He did, and he looked damn good too. B was a lot lighter than what I was used to. He was the same complexion as Drake, with a nice ass goatee and a low haircut. His eyes were almond-shaped and brown, accompanied by long ass eyelashes I'd die for. His lips were thin and always moist–begging to be kissed, but I'd never. Not yet at least. He was around 5'6 and slim; slimmer than what I like, but he was attractive nonetheless.

"About time you made it here, ho! I was missing you," yelled Jai as she staggered toward me, pulling her short bodycon dress down.

I hugged her, "Bitch, you lifted. What you drinking on?"

"A little bit of everything. All top shelf, bitch! I've been spending all Ryan's ugly ass money," she whispered in my ear, and then laughed.

"Don't start that shit tonight, sis. His money ain't ugly, remember?"

"Hell fuck nah it ain't," yelled Jai as she draped her arm over my shoulder.

"Chill out for a minute though, sis. You drove?"

"Yeah I did, but you know I'm the best drunk designated driver on Earth," she winked, "I'll be straight."

I told her to give me her keys. Bitch wasn't driving home like that. Hell nah. If something happened, I'd never be able to live with the guilt. She was reluctant and told me to relax, but I planned on grabbing her keys without her knowing it.

I ordered me an Amaretto Sour and sipped as I sat in my seat dancing to the music. The bar was more like a club. Delux banged like this every Saturday. B stood behind me and wrapped his arms around me. I smiled as he whispered lame shit in my ear. His corniness was cute, to be honest.

"You really be laying it on thick, B," I looked at him, "What is your name?"

He licked his lips and sat beside me, "Branden."

"Branden is a lot better than B," I said before taking a sip of my drink, "Trust."

He rubbed his chin, "You think so?"

I nodded, "I know so. Don't tell anybody else your name is B. Use Branden at all times," I winked at him.

"You're so down to Earth, and cool as fuck. Why are you single?"

I sat there thinking about his question before answering. I was single for a number of reasons. For one, niggas didn't appreciate a woman like me. I stayed with my ex through it all, and he treated me like shit. I always thought I could change him but in reality, if a nigga ain't ready to change, there's nothing you can do about that. You can suck him, fuck him, and feed him. You can cater to his every need, but if he's not ready to grow up and commit to you, he won't. It took me a minute, but I finally realized it. I was bending myself over backwards to please him, and it was never enough. Eventually, I realized that I was too much of a good bitch to deal with what I dealt with. It felt good to be free from him, but I can't lie and say I didn't miss the good times.

"I'm single because my ex didn't know how to appreciate me," I replied.

He grabbed my hand and kissed my knuckles, "If you let me Storm, I'll show you just how you deserve to be treated."

I wanted to believe him, but Branden had wandering eyes and I saw straight through his bullshit. He talked a good game, but the shit wasn't sincere. I just smiled at him. Good thing I wasn't a stupid gullible bitch. Otherwise, I would've fucked Branden a long time ago.

"Come dance with me sis," yelled Jai as she danced towards me.

I sat my drink down and met her half way, giggling, "Bitch you bout drunk as fuck!"

"Yaaaas. And I feel good too. Don't forget to mention I'm bout bad as fuck too! Ain't no bitch in here fucking with us!" she yelled, as she grabbed my hands and waved them in the air.

Us Against Everybody: Miss Candice

[CHAPTER SIX]
VICE

I took a shot of Patrón and asked the bartender for another one. I was out with my nigga Reek at this little bar downtown. My mood was sour as fuck and I really didn't want to be out, but the bitch at my crib was taking me there. I tried to put her ignorant ass up in a hotel, but she rapped about the bed bug epidemic. Apparently she was paranoid, because she had to move out of her crib because of them. That's the only reason her petty ass was at my crib.

Joslyn was really playing on the possibility of being pregnant. I didn't even think the bitch was pregnant, to be honest. She took a piss test and it came back negative, but she's so bent on being pregnant that she made an appointment with her doctor and took a blood test earlier. After her appointment, we went to Somerset because she burned all of her clothes and needed some new shit. That's how I ran into brown skin.

I had no idea she worked at Neiman's. When I peeped her little sexy ass at the cash register, I wanted to grab her and take her away but shorty wasn't happy to see me. Joslyn rapped in her ear about being pregnant and shit. I didn't look like anything but a liar to her, especially since I didn't hit her up twenty minutes after I left like I promised. Some shit popped off and when I got around to calling her, I couldn't get through to her. Lil mama put me on the block list, and I couldn't blame her. That's why I didn't even step to her when I saw her come in the bar.

"You think shit straight over there by now," asked Reek, referring to the problem that came up earlier.

"Let's give it a few days. Let shit cool down, then we'll open up shop," I replied after downing another shot and watching Storm as she danced with Jai.

One of my dope spots got hit, and I lost a nice amount of drugs and money. DPD had a hard-on for me. They wanted me bad, but they couldn't touch me. They might've had my shit, but they wouldn't be satisfied until I was behind bars. The fuck I look like kicking back in a dope spot? They will never get hands on me by moving stupidly like that. Fuck niggas even pull me over every chance they get, hoping to find something on me. Never. I'm not a stupid nigga. The fuck I look like riding around with illegal shit on me? I'm not a stupid nigga. I take extreme measures to make sure I'll never see the inside of a jail cell.

"You think somebody talking?" he asked.

"Most likely. It won't be hard for me to get my hands on 'em." I paused, "Ay, what time is it? It's about time we handle that Lando problem."

Reek nodded to the entrance, "He just walked in, bro."

Every time we went to handle the nigga, it was bad timing, but now was perfect. He was already drunk, staggering around with his bum ass niggas. He didn't even notice me when he walked by yelling at one of the waitresses. His boys didn't peep me neither. There were five of them, and just me and Reek. Our murder game was sick, so it would be nothing to take them niggas out.

"Well damn, look at God," I said with a chuckle, "Brought that nigga straight to us."

Reek laughed and slapped hands with me, "Right place, right time bro."

I nodded as I watched him take a seat at the end of the bar. He was posted, and so was I. I wasn't moving until he did. As soon as the opportunity presented itself, I was sending bullets straight through his big ass dome. Fuck 'em.

My beef with Orlando ran long; shit, back to grade school if you want to be technical. He's always tried to compete with me, from fucking with the same bitches to rocking the same type of clothes. The nigga stayed tryin' to outshine me, but nothing he did worked. I've always been that nigga.

The problem now is he keeps opening up spots in my territory. I told the nigga to tread lightly. I warned him, but no matter how many times I had my niggas run up in his shit, another one popped up. The disrespect's been going on for about a month. It's about time for me to show this nigga that it's best to respect me. I told him I would come see him. I guess he didn't believe me. My word was bond–believe that. These niggas have a hard time believing that. I never make a promise I can't keep.

"How you wanna go about shit, bro?" asked Reek as he eyed Orlando.

"Stop staring. Follow my lead, my nigga. I don't want to discuss the shit here. Eyes and ears all around this bitch." I started to take another shot, but stopped and pushed the glass aside, "Just know the niggas getting handled tonight."

I didn't want to get drunk. That was my exact intention before Orlando popped up. Shit, I had to be drunk to deal with Jos. But, nah, I had shit to handle. I couldn't be out here sloppy drunk trying to off a nigga. That's how people fucked up, and I didn't have room for anymore fuck ups. I dealt with enough of those last year.

Last year was crazy as hell for me and my squad. Last year was the reason why the DPD wanted me so bad now. I was knocked, but I had me a legit ass lawyer who got me off because of a few flaws in the evidence they had against me. Plus, their key witness was murdered a week before trial. The fuck did niggas think? That I wouldn't find out? Vice always found out. Vice might act like he don't know what's what but trust, a nigga was always hip. What happened to the witness back then is what got niggas so shook now. I mean, as usual, there is one who feels as if they can't escape the inevitable, but of course, it's impossible. Whoever is talking now will be dealt with accordingly.

Anyway, back then my spots were being hit left and right. The boys illegally bugged my crib and cars, which is one of the reasons the case was thrown out. Plus, I never talked directly. I never said the words drugs, crack, coke, or any of that dumb shit. All they had was 'translations' given to them by this one stupid nigga named Erik. Erik ended up being a dead-end–a dead-end left for dead, at a dead-end street; symbolic for exactly what he was – a dead-end. I smiled when the prosecutor announced that their key, and only, witness was murdered. Without him, there was nothing they could do.

Reek tapping me on the arm killed my train of thought, "Ay, ain't that ol girl you was kicking it with at the Riverwalk that day?"

I looked in her direction and I'd be damned. She was smiling as Lando spat game in her ear. I smirked, "Hell yeah, let me see yo phone real quick bro."

Reek handed me his phone, and I retrieved mines. I looked her up and dialed her number into Reek's phone. I watched her fumble around in her purse, then excuse herself from Lando as she walked away towards the restrooms. I stood up and followed her, being as low key as possible. I didn't want Orlando to know we were even in the bar.

I hung up just as she answered, and we turned the corner that led right to the restrooms. When she turned around to head back to the dance floor, she literally bumped into me. I grabbed her and pulled her into the men's room. She tried to pull away from me, but I held her tightly and locked the door.

"Um, let me go. What type of shit are you on," she huffed with her perfectly arched eyebrows frowned up.

I buried my head in her neck and got high off her intoxicating, womanly scent, "You smell good as fuck, lil' mama."

Storm beat me on the chest, "Let me go! I'm on a date and you are way out of line. I don't even know you! You on some rape shit."

I let her go and stood there laughing, "You don't know me, but seriously? You think I'll rape you, lil' mama? Come on now."

She ran her fingers through her hair, "What do you want, liar?"

I held my chest like I was hurt, "Liar? Me? Nah, not I. You never gave me a chance to explain myself."

Storm shook her head, "What you have to say doesn't even matter, Vice. Besides, like I said, I'm on a date."

I leaned on the bathroom door, "With who?"

"None of your business," she replied with her arms folded over her chest.

"Orlando?"

"Who?"

"Nigga who was just in your ear," I replied, trying not to sound like a crazy nigga.

She laughed, "Lando is my childhood friend. How you know him?"

"Not important. Whoever you here with gon' be pissed."

"Any why is that?"

"Because he's wasting his time."

She laughed and asked me what I meant. I told her she'd be mine in a few weeks. Although she wanted to be friends, I knew she'd eventually be mine. That's how life was for me. If I saw something or someone I wanted, I got it. No matter what lengths I had to go, I always got what I wanted, and who I

71

wanted more than anything right now was this feisty, sexy brown skin that goes by Storm. Fuck all that friend shit. I was going to show her that I wasn't the liar she thought I was–as soon as I got rid of Joslyn's messy ass.

Storm laughed it off and turned to unlock the door. I stopped her and grabbed hold of her.

"Let me go, crazy. I told you I'm on a date."

"Never, lil' mama. It's something about you. I'm not letting you go," I replied figuratively.

She blushed, "You...I don't even know what to say. But seriously, Vice, I'm being rude. He's been texting me."

I let her go, "Aight, he can borrow you for now. I know what it is, and what its gon' be."

Storm rolled her eyes with a smile, "Enjoy the rest of your night, Vice."

"Oh, I definitely will. You...you don't enjoy yours too much. On the real lil' mama, take yo ass home after this."

She cracked up laughing and told me I wasn't her daddy. I, in return, said I might not be but eventually I'd be something close to it. She blew me off again, and we went our separate ways. I watched her walk over to the bar and sit next to a lame. The way she smiled with him was different. It was off. The smiles she gave me were genuine; now they were forced on. I had lil' mama. She wasn't feeling that corny ass dude for real, and that made a nigga's confidence shoot sky high.

An hour later, the bar was closing and people were heading to their vehicles. Me and Reek were already posted in the whip, peeping the scenery, and keeping an eye out for Orlando and his crew. Hook was deep as fuck so, off top, I knew the hit couldn't be done out here. It's cool though, I liked creeping up on niggas. There's nothing like the element of surprise. I'm not too fond of gunfights. If I could easily and inconspicuously get rid of all my enemies, I would, but the murder game ain't always that simple.

Reek hit me on the shoulder, "Check his weak ass out, bro."

I took my eyes off Storm and placed them on Orlando, who was standing at his whip, whispering in some ugly girl's ear, who had a sick ass body.

I turned my attention back to Storm, who appeared to be walking around trying to find Jai. Niggas were getting rowdy, despite the fact that the boys were posted and circling all around this bitch, so I needed lil' mama to hop in the whip and get the fuck out of dodge. I'd hate for her to get caught up in the middle of some mess.

I unplugged my phone from the AUX and called her up. I knew she had to have removed me from the block list by now.

And I was right.

"Yeah," she answered, obviously annoyed.

"I thought I told you to go home."

Storm sucked her teeth, "What you want boy? And why are you stalking me, crazy?"

"I want you to go home," I seriously replied. "Why are you walking around out here alone, after two in the morning like won't nobody snatch yo lil sexy ass up?"

"I'm looking for Jai," she replied before sighing.

"Where's your date?"

"I can't seem to find him neither. I went to the restroom and when I came out, the bar was emptying."

I shifted my eyes toward Orlando, who was still in homegirl's ear. I couldn't focus on her well-being while trying to handle this bitch nigga.

Reek gave me a look, as if to ask what was up. I put my finger up telling him to wait.

"Storm, you need to go home."

"Not without Jai...oh, there her drunk ass go. Where you at?"

"Kicking back. Ay, take care of yourself shorty. Hit me up when you touch down at the crib, aight?"

"Okay," she paused, "why do you care so much?"

"Because I do. And cut that weak ass nigga off for leaving you out here by yourself," I said before we ended the call.

"You really feeling sexy lil' brown skin, huh?" asked Reek with a smirk.

I glanced at him, then shifted the car into drive, "Fuck yeah. I know a good one when I see one, and lil' mama is as legit as they come, bro."

I peeped Lando hop in his whip with ol girl beside him. Nigga was on a pussy mission; not thinking, not paying attention to shit but the pussy sitting beside him. Distracted is how I liked my targets. I kept my distance as I followed him to where I assume was his bitch's crib. He was riding in the opposite direction of the hood.

Reek passed me the blunt, and I took a pull from it. I was still feeling the liq, and the Cush was going to mellow me out just like I needed.

75

I turned the volume to the stereo up and bobbed my head to Future and Drake rapping about how fake mothafuckas are. Soon as a nigga start stacking bread, everybody wanna come out the woodworks. Nobody was around for the struggle. I could relate like a mothafucka to the track.

Where them niggas was at when I had to struggle? Where them niggas was at when I had to turn to selling dope? Niggas wasn't giving a fuck about me then. I was a low key, solo nigga but as soon as I started stacking bread, pushing whips, and making a name for myself out here, niggas wanted to come out the woodwork. Asking for handouts and shit. I didn't even fuck with most of my family because of that. I looked out for auntie and my cousin Dawson, but fuck everybody else.

Where yo ass was at dog when niggas wasn't feeding me?
Where yo ass was at dog when bitches didn't need me?
Where yo ass was at dog when niggas tried to run off?

Just as I was about to head down memory lane, Lando parked in the driveway of a small brick house. We were on the West side off Livernois. I parked the whip about four houses down and grabbed the burner out the middle compartment. Reek tossed me a ski mask before putting his on himself. I stared at it and decided I didn't want to wear it. I wanted this nigga to see who was taking him out the game.

I tossed it in the backseat, and Reek looked at me like I was crazy, "Bro, you need that. He got a bitch with him."

I checked the bullets in the gun and glanced at him, "And you think that bitch will be stupid enough to snitch? Shit, we can take her out the game too if need be."

"Mannnn, put the skully on bro," said Reek, shaking his head full of twisted up dreads, "You a crazy nigga, I swear."

I might be crazy. That just might be true.

Reek reached to the backseat and handed it to me. I snatched it from him and put it on. I really didn't want to have to kill home girl. So yeah, I needed it.

We crept out of the car and crotched as we made our way to the house. Orlando was standing behind thick-and-ugly as she unlocked the door to her crib, just as we crept up on the porch. They never seen us coming. Orlando was too busy pressing his body up on her, and she was too busy trying to get inside.

As soon as she opened the door, we ambushed them. We put the gun on them and pushed them inside. Off rip, home girl started with the waterworks.

I told her to sit her ass on the couch, and she did. Orlando stood there, eyes switching from me to Reek. He had a burner on him, and was thinking of the perfect time to pull it. No time was perfect. Fuck I look like allowing some stupid shit like that to happen?

I hit Orlando with the butt of the gun and he fell to the floor, grabbing his jaw.

"Aahh, fuck! Do you niggas know who you fucking with? Dog, I got niggas all around the D."
I squatted beside him and lifted my ski mask, "Talk that shit to another cat. Stop fronting like you got pull out here, pussy."

Orlando threw his head back, "Ah come on now, V—"

I stuck the gun in his mouth midsentence and said, "Watch your mouth, fuck nigga."

I removed it and he continued, "Shit ain't even this serious, nigga! Over some hoods?! Why can't we all just get bread, nigga? We can break bread together."

He was pleading and trying to do business with a nigga who didn't give a fuck about 'em. He was wasting his breath, and I let him know that.

"You talking for no reason, Lando. I don't break bread with stupid niggas."

He held his hands up, "Come on now ma—"

I blew his brains out, and ol' girls screams echoed through my ears as Reek tried to keep her calm. I leaned down and looked at Orlando. I ignored the big ass hole in the middle of his forehead and stared into his eyes. Every man I offed showed a weakness when it was their time to go. Lando ran around the hood acting like a tough nigga, but when it came time for him to meet his maker, he turned into a straight up pussy. Nigga basically begged for his life.

That's the difference between me and these fuck niggas. If a nigga come at me with the burner on me, I'm going to be the same dude I've always been. What the hell I look like begging another man for life? What the hell I look like going out like anything other than the boss ass nigga that I am?

"Bro, we gotta go," yelled Reek.

I looked over my shoulder, "What happened to her?"

Reek looked down at ol' girl, who was laid out on the floor, "Knocked the bitch out, she wouldn't shut the fuck up."

I stood up and nodded, "We out."

Us Against Everybody: Miss Candice

[CHAPTER SEVEN]
JAI

I laid there trying to think of how to get away from this nigga. Ryan had his arms wrapped around me, breathing his stank ass morning breath on my neck. He was already pussy whipped, and he only hit the cat once. I should've known better fucking him so soon, but the nigga bread run long, and rent is due. I have other guys, but I knew I could get the most from Ryan because he's a newbie and is still in awe–in awe of my bad ass, of course. I told you, he's ugly. Ugly niggas dish out the most bread when they fucking with a baddie like me.

I sighed and tried to wiggle free, but he held me tighter. His ass didn't want to let me go. What? He thought I'd leave and never come back or some shit? That's how he was acting. I sighed again and tried to move his big, muscular arm.

"Where you trying to go, baby?" asked Ryan out of his sleep.

"I have to pee."

He moved his arms and said, "The bathroom is down the hall on the right."

I got out of bed and walked my naked ass to the bathroom. I left the bar with him last night. I was drunk as fuck when we got to his crib, so ain't no telling what type of freak shit I was on to have him so attached already. Knowing me, I probably went all out. Probably damn near sucked the skin off his dick. His dick...shit, I didn't even know if we used a rubber or not. Ryan is a pretty put together nigga, so I'm sure he made sure jimmy was on extra tight. Speaking of his dick though, I do have one distinct memory. That mothafucka is big as hell. Damn. Thick and long. His dick has to be almost a foot long. Subway sandwich ass dick!

I laughed as I sat on the toilet and pissed. His place is nice too. Although he lives on campus at MSU, he has a condo downtown Detroit. I need to know how he gets his money. The nigga ain't broke by a long shot and for some reason, I didn't get the drug dealer vibe from him.

I wiped, flushed, and washed my hands before heading back to his room. Not before snooping a little first. I walked around his condo looking for nothing in particular. The place was clean as fuck for it to belong to a man. Ryan's a clean cut dude but still, for his crib to be this spotless? It looked like a bitch cleaned it. I didn't care. I was just saying. If his ass do have a bitch, I need to know. I don't need to be posted up in bed with him and some broad bust through. If he got a chick, I won't care. I just need to be put up on game and shit.

I saw a few pieces of mail on the coffee table and fingered through it. Nothing but bills and junk. A couple seconds later, Ryan called out for me, causing me to jump. I was holding a picture of him and some female and damn near dropped it.

"Here I come," I replied as I put the picture back where I found it.

When I made it back to the room, he was sitting on side of the bed rubbing sleep from his eyes, with his back to me. Seeing him from this angle, you would think he was a nice looking guy. His back was ripped up and full of tats. He had the build of a professional football player. That's what he was aspiring to be, and he fit the description perfectly.

"What took you so long?" he asked, turning to me exposing that ugly ass face.

It took everything in me not to frown up at him. Shit, I know I might sound like a shallow ass bitch and so what. It is what it is. I'm only fucking with him because his money ain't ugly. Tuh! Bills are at a continuous flow, and it sure don't seem like the cash will be slowing up anytime soon, so I put a smile on my face and hugged him from behind. I wrapped my legs around him and kissed his neck.

"I was being nosey," I honestly replied. "Do you have a woman I should be worried about?"

He looked over his shoulder at me, "No, why do you ask?"

"The picture on the mantel."

He tensed up, "Ex broad."

"What happened?"

He pulled me on his lap and I straddled him, looking into his eyes.

"I found out she was using me. She didn't care about a nigga. I can't deal with those type of women. I left her. I despise everything about a gold digger," Ryan sternly replied.

I cleared my throat and blinked, "Why do you have the picture then?"

"It's a reminder of how stupid I was. A reminder that I'll never let myself fall in love with another gold digging broad."

I hugged him and laid my head on his shoulder. Damn! Ryan ain't as much of a pushover like I expected. I definitely had to play my cards right now. This nigga was serious as fuck right now. I'd never heard him speak so seriously. He was about that shit. Whoever that dumb bitch was who got found out was not about to fuck this up for me! I was a pro when it came to this paper chasing shit.

I looked down at my tattoo on my wrist that read *Gold Digger*, and prayed like fuck that he hadn't noticed it. I made a mental note to cover it with makeup whenever we were around each other. I didn't need shit fucking this up for me. Hell, I was happy the nigga wasn't from the hood, because he wouldn't have given me the time of day and I didn't need that right now. What I needed was to get into this nigga's head, heart, and most definitely pockets. I'd do whatever was absolutely necessary–which is why I lowered my body to the floor.

I parted his legs and held his dick in my hands, while staring him in the eyes. My look was seductive and by the look of Ryan's face, I had him exactly where I needed him. I smiled and wrapped my full lips around his thick dick. He threw his head back and let out a low grunt. As I sucked him, I slowly stroked it. He was in euphoric bliss. If it was one thing I was good at, it was getting men to do exactly what I needed them to do. Ryan might be talking all of that 'no gold digger' shit now, but what he hasn't met is a bitch like me. I play my role, and I plays it well!

Us Against Everybody: Miss Candice

[CHAPTER EIGHT]
VICE

A nigga could appreciate waking up to the smell of breakfast, but I needed this bitch to get the fuck on. I made it back to the crib at four in the morning, and the time on my phone now read 10:17AM. I wasn't tripping about waking up too early. I was tripping because she was making herself at home. Little did she know, I was about to nip that shit in the bud right now.

I sat up on side of the bed and rubbed the sleep from my eyes. I sat there a minute, going through my phone, read a few text messages, and responded to the important ones. As usual, I had a busy ass day ahead of me. Before heading to the kitchen, I texted Reek to let him know I'd be heading his way in about three hours.

When I made it to the kitchen, Joslyn was prancing around naked, stacking food on plates. I grabbed the remote to the sound bar and turned the voice of Nicki Minaj off.

"Good morning, Vice," said Joslyn with a smile as I took a seat at the kitchen island.

I nodded at her, "What's all of this?"

She shrugged and sat a plate of pancakes, sausages, grits, and eggs in front of me, "I just wanted to show some appreciation for all you've done for me."

I took a bite of a sausage link, "You heard from the lab yet?"

Her face turned beet red. She didn't want to talk about those test results. I couldn't understand what was up with her. Seemed like since she's noticed how into Storm I was, she wanted to stay a part of my life. Couple months ago, Jos was a totally different broad. She felt threatened by Storm, and I understood completely.

Joslyn wiped her hands on a towel, "You're welcome Vice. Damn, why everything gotta be about this pregnancy?"

"Yeah, thank you for cooking food from my refrigerator, Jos. Thanks a lot, ma." I took a sip of my apple juice, "A nigga ain't being unappreciative of the food. Shit's bomb, aight? And everything is about that 'pregnancy'. Shit ain't been on for us like that in months. Have you heard from the lab Joslyn?"

She rolled her eyes and sat across from me, "Yeah, but I want a second opinion."

I laughed and wiped my mouth, "Fuck out of here Joslyn. You ain't pregnant ma." I ate a spoon of grits, "You got two days to get your shit together, aight?"

"Why are you being so nasty? God. Yeah, the test came back negative, but I still haven't had a period. Something's going on."

"Well it ain't pregnancy, shorty." I stood up and finished off the rest of my food, "Do something constructive with your time today, girl. Like, apartment searching. A nigga ain't joking about you having two days. You ain't my responsibility anymore, Joslyn."

"Where you going?"

I laughed, "Did you hear anything I said? You. Gotta. Dip."

She stood up and got in my face, "I can't stand you! I swear to God."

I looked down and patted her on the cheek, "Keep calm, before I throw your ass out right now, Joslyn. Don't forget to clean up your mess."

I walked away, ignoring the crocodile tears she was spilling. I didn't give a fuck. The test came back negative. Joslyn wasn't my problem. I couldn't give a fuck less about where she went, but she had to get the fuck up out of my spot.

Hours later, I pulled up in front of Reek's place in my cocaine white Audi, blasting Big Sean's Paradise. We had a few runs to make. A couple niggas to see. A few bitch made niggas to check. It was a regular day in the hood. Unlike me, Reek still stayed in the D off Seven Mile and Gratiot. I stayed posted up over here though. Most of my spots were in this hood. I kept an eye on my money. I had to.

I pulled my phone from the pocket of my blue jean True Religion shorts and scrolled down my contact list until I got to her name.

Me (3:23PM): Can you be ready in a couple hours?

Storm (3:24PM): Ready for what? Hi to you, too Vice.

Me (3:24PM): Ready for our date.

Storm (3:26PM): our date?

Me (3:27PM): I'll be there in about two, three hours, lil mama.

Storm (3:28PM): You don't even know where 'there' is LOL.

Me (3:28PM): like I said, I'll be there in two hours.

I didn't know where 'there' was, but I intended to find out later. I could've just asked her, but I'd rather get the information from Jai so a nigga can look like the boss type cat I am. Storm didn't want a relationship with me, so I had to do everything in my power to persuade her to think otherwise.

Reek hopped in the whip and gave me a five, "Wassup brodie? What's on the agenda today?"

"Same ol' shit," I sped off, "Did last night make the news yet?"

Reek nodded and fired up a blunt, "Fuck yeah. Ol' girl ain't talking about shit. She told them boys it was an attempted robbery gone wrong."

I nodded and made a left on Seven Mile, "Any noise from them fuck niggas?"

He nodded again, "The hood talking. Matter fact, I think we should swing through that bitch."

I looked at him with a smirk, "Where you think I'm headed, nigga?"

I didn't like any drama with bitches I fucked with but, I didn't mind knocking a few niggas off. I didn't mind intimidating dudes. I actually liked it. A lot of dudes liked talking behind my back. Niggas did the shit all day. I enjoyed walking up on conversations about me. I enjoyed watching weak niggas cur up. I didn't let it faze me none.

I peeped Jai walking out of Captain Jay's Chicken and made a quick right into the parking lot. She was getting in the car with some nigga just as I hopped out of mine. Reek asked me what was up because he thought the beef was on. I told him shit was good with a simple hand gesture.

I walked up to my man's car and leaned in the passenger window. He looked at me like I was crazy.

"Wassup, dog," I said to him before addressing Jai, "I need brown skin's address."

"What? Nigga I can't give you her address," replied Jai with an attitude.

"Yes you can," I adjusted my shorts before kneeling down, "Peep, lil' mama already know I'm coming through. Hit me off with the address, Jai."

She shook her head and glanced at her dude, "Why didn't you get it from her then, Vice?"

"Because I want it from you." She paused, and I noticed her guy getting agitated, "Tell her to give me the address and I'm out of y'all hair. I swear, my guy."

Jai sucked her teeth, "You lucky I fucks with you, Vice."

"Yeah, aight," I handed her my phone, "Put it in there."

She took it and typed Storm's address in, "You better not do anything to my girl."

I frowned at her, "Be real. Fuck you mean?" I snatched the phone from her and walked away from the car.

I hopped back in my whip and saved her address to my navi. I felt Reek staring at me. Bro wasn't used to me tripping over a broad like I was. I looked at him and shrugged as I pulled off. He took a pull from his blunt and said I was pussy whipped and I ain't even smelled the pussy. I laughed and said fuck him. I didn't have the pussy yet, but I planned on sliding up in that pretty soon. Storm was too sexy not to aspire to fuck. Any nigga with two eyes could see that.

I pushed shorty in the back of mind and focused on the situation at hand. I made a left turn on Robinwood St. and slowed up. I cruised on the block that once belonged to Lando. He wasn't serving shit over here–fuck no, this was my hood, but the nigga did stay over here. The block was full of his people. Pouring up, blasting music, talking a bunch of shit. They were showing love for the nigga I murked. I was a ballzy ass nigga for even rolling through here, but like I've always said, I just don't give a fuck.

Reek passed me the blunt and said, "This bitch sewed up bro. Maybe we should get the fuck out of dodge."

I took a pull from the blunt and glanced at him, "What for nigga? You worried?" I inhaled the smoke and said, "Fuck these niggas."

I passed him the blunt back and lowered my window. I got looks from niggas. Mean mugs. Niggas wanted me dead, but you know what I did? I smiled and nodded at them. I loved taunting mothafuckas. I did this because despite it all, these niggas weren't going to jump stupid. Not out here in front of a block full of women and children. I wanted to get these boys riled up.

I slowed up in front of Lando's old house. His OG, baby mamas, cousins...shit, his whole family was posted on the porch.

I turned my music down and said, "Sorry for your loss, Mrs. Willis."

Orlando's brothers and cousins ran down the porch. I shifted the whip in park quick as fuck, and before they could reach my car, Reek and I were standing outside of the car. I held my hands up, "Whoa, whoa, what's the issue dog?"

"Get the fuck away from here! You Devil! Get away from our home!" yelled Mrs. Willis, crying her eyes out. She was frantic, shaking and barely standing.

One of Orlando's old bitches grabbed her and pulled her into the house.

"Get the fuck from over here yo. I swear to God, I will lay you out right here nigga," threatened Orlando's big brother Tank.

I held my chin up and smirked, "Do what you wanna do, my mans."

Reek walked on my side of the car and patted his waist, "Wrong time and place. Fuck with us another time."

I glanced at Reek, "We can get it popping right now, bro. Fuck you mean?"

I was tripping. Making these niggas mad. You know how I get down. I didn't lay the murder game down in front of kids, and these niggas didn't neither. I didn't think they did. I mean, what nigga with half a heart would? If one of these pussy niggas wanna take it there, I won't hesitate, but I won't pull the burner out in front of a child.

"Just get the fuck on, Vice," said Tank. "I'll see you in these streets."

I looked around, "We in the streets now."

Reek shook his head and said, "Too many kids out to this bitch, bro."

I just looked at him. I turned my attention back to Tank, and his fists were balled.

"You wanna knock a nigga out huh, cuz?" I smiled, "Make a move."

Tank shook his head and turned to walk away, "Another time and place, bitch nigga. Another time and place," He looked at me over his shoulder, "I will see you."

"Of course you'll see me, pussy, I own these streets." I replied before getting back in the whip.

As soon as Reek got in, he started to run his mouth, "Fuck was that all about, brodie?"

I shifted the car in drive and sped off, "I do what the fuck I want, my nigga."

He started to say something else, but I turned the stereo back up. I just wanted to intimidate them niggas. I wanted to get their blood boiling. They were already mad enough, and me pulling up only made them madder. I wanted them mad. I wanted blood to be spilled all over the streets of Seven Mile. I wasn't tripping, because I knew that blood wouldn't belong to me. Maybe a few niggas I rolled with, but not mine. My aim was too accurate; my murder game too strong. I wasn't going to stop until I had the blood of all of Orlando's associates on my hands. Literally. Them weak ass niggas wanted to test my gangsta by setting up shop on my blocks like I wouldn't touch 'em. Well, it was game time.

Us Against Everybody: Miss Candice

[CHAPTER NINE]
STORM

I've got to admit, I love his assertiveness. Still, I don't really want to fuck with him on any level besides friendship. To be real, I needed to stay the hell away from him. Not only because I wasn't sure if I'd be able to protect my heart, but because I had a feeling he killed Orlando. We weren't the best of friends; shit, we barely talked, but it was still sad.

Orlando was murdered last night. I kept thinking of how Vice questioned me about Lando being in my ear, and when I asked him how they knew each other, he changed the subject. I didn't really know how Vice really got down, but Jai had vouched for his craziness numerous times. When I asked her why she gave him my address knowing he was a looney toon ass nigga, she said because she'd never seen him so pressed over a woman and knew he didn't have ill intentions.

Now I'm standing at my walk-in closet, trying to decide on what to wear. As childish as it may seem, I need help. As much as I don't want to have some type of feelings for Vice, I can't help but. He's intriguing, captivating, enticing, but yet intimidating. There's something about the 'boss' in him that makes me drawn to him. I hate the shit, because I already know there's hella drama attached to him.

Since my mama lived too far and Jai was all the way in the D, I decided on a blue jean romper and some cute wedge sandals. This should be cute enough, right? I don't even know where this boy is taking me.

After I showered, I stood in my full-length mirror getting dressed. I couldn't help but notice the rapid beating of my heart. I leaned over and placed both of my palms on the wall, trying to control what felt like an anxiety attack. What the fuck is this?

The ringing of my phone scared me. I flinched and turned around to grab it off my bed. The name staring back at me caused my heart to beat faster. Is this nigga doing this to me? I've never felt anything like this before. The shit scared me. I didn't know if I should run or what?

I slid the green phone over and said, "Hello?"

"Ready or not, I'll be pulling up in ten seconds, lil' mama."

I hurried to the mirror and fingered through my loose wand curls. I grabbed my MAC Siss lipstick off my vanity and applied another coat.

"I'm ready," I paused, "Where are you taking me?"

"Aight, good. I'm outside, beauty," said Vice before hanging up.

I stood there looking at the phone for a second. *Did this nigga really just hang up in my face?* Instead of being mad, I smiled. He's different, and I like that about him. Sometimes he comes off as rude, but I just think that's the boss in him.

I grabbed my Michael Kors bag off my vanity, checked my makeup one last time, and headed out. When I opened the door, there he stood looking better than I could ever remember. He held a bouquet of red and white roses, adorned by baby breath flowers. Vice was dressed casually in some designer cargo shorts held up by a Gucci belt, and a white Polo top. On his feet were a pair of white Louboutin gym shoes.

Vice smiled at me, exposing one dimpled cheek and crispy white teeth, "Wassup Lil' mama? You looking mighty fine this evening." He handed me the flowers and boldly pulled me into his arms.

I wasn't used to such assertiveness, but damn it felt good to be in his arms. As he hugged me, I inhaled the intoxicating scent of his Gucci Guilty Black cologne. This man was too damn irresistible. It was like my intentions of keeping shit friendly went out the window as soon as I laid my eyes on his sparkling hazels. The way the lightness of his eyes complimented his caramel complexion drove me crazy. He was damn near perfect–in looks at least.

"And you...you look nice too, Vice," I replied, stammering over my words, "Thank you for the roses. They're pretty. Let me go put them in the house."

I went to pull away from him, but he held me tighter and effortlessly lifted me from my feet. He's damn near six feet, and I'm barely five feet. He held me close to his body and smelled my neck.

"Damn lil' mama..." was all he said while I dangled in his arms full of confusion, but interest.

He was bold. Blunt. Qualities in a man that I'm not used to. I'm used to dudes like Branden. Those who constantly run game and try to impress me. I didn't get that feel from Vice. He was genuine, although he seemed to be very into me. It wasn't forced on though. He didn't come off phony. Everything – even him picking me up – felt normal, like I was supposed to be in his arms.

Finally he put me down, but his boldness didn't stop there. He stared into my eyes and for a second there, I forgot all about my plans of taking the flowers in the crib. His eye contact held me in captivity. His eye contact was magnetic, and like a positive connecting to a negative, my body was drawn to him. Without recognition as to what I was doing, I inched in closer to him. We were already close to begin with, but now, if I was taller, we'd literally be face-to-face.

Vice leaned down and grabbed hold of my chin. I closed my eyes, anticipating a kiss, but it never happened. He slowly, but softly brushed his lips against mine before telling me how beautiful I was. Like a teenaged girl, I blushed and thanked him.

I cleared my throat and turned to go back into the house. He grabbed my arm and said, "I apologize if I overstepped boundaries, lil' mama." He held his hands up, "I ain't a creep or shit like that, shorty."

I laughed, "You sure you ain't a creep? I mean, should I even be leaving with you? To a place I'm still unaware of," I joked to lighten the mood a little, but he didn't even crack a smile.

"I'd never hurt you, Storm. And if you allow me, I'd like to show you just how much I mean that."

He was asking me to be his girl, but as much as I wanted to be that to him, I knew I didn't need to go there with him. I wanted to, bad as fuck, but the red flags wouldn't let me. Hell, the red flags should've sent me running in the other direction but like I said, the magnetism to him was pulling me in his direction. Like a positive to a negative...

I smiled, "Vice..."

He stuffed his hands in his pockets and cocked his head back a little, "I'm not leaving this doorstep without you as my girl, brown skin."

I started to say something, but he interrupted me again.

He pulled his hand from his pocket and looked down at his watch, which was adorned in diamonds and said, "I'm a busy nigga but ay, fuck it."

I walked into the house and sat the vase of roses on my coffee table. My heart started to beat fast again, and I took a couple deep breaths. It was him. It had to be because of him. My attraction to him was just as strong as he displayed his attraction for me. I've never been this into a man. I've never feared not being a part of someone's life. Yeah, I didn't want us to end and we hadn't even began.

Vice was a straight to the point, direct dude. He wanted me, and he wasn't taking no as an answer. I didn't want to tell him no, but I needed to–right? I mean shit, this nigga was living a life my mother stressed with my daddy about. She literally had to beg him to stop the bullshit. Pops didn't stop the thug life until they were divorced, and even then, he only stopped because he ended up spending a few years behind bars, and when he got out he couldn't get back on.

I left the house and locked the door, all while avoiding eye contact with Vice. He stood there watching my every move. When I turned to him, our eyes locked and I had to quickly look away before I was stuck there. His eye contact was just that intense.

"Alright, I'm ready. Where we going," I said as I started to leave the porch. He stayed there though. I rolled my eyes, "Vice."

He turned towards me and said, "I already told you what was up."

I drew my lips in my mouth then said, "And what if I don't change my mind about only being friends, Vice?"

He shrugged, "A nigga got enough friends. I'm sweet on that, lil' mama."

I made a sound of frustration, "Why are yo—"

"What are you so afraid of?" asked Vice, slowly approaching me, "Clearly a nigga really feeling you. I ain't going through all of this to get you, fuck up, and lose you. Stop rejecting me knowing damn well you want me." Bluntness. Boldness. He never bit his tongue. I found that out the first day we met. He said what was on his mind, no matter what.

I ran my hands through my hair, "This is unfair."

He stood before me and grabbed hold of my hands, "What's unfair is the fact that you want to flaunt all of this beauty in my face, talking about friendship," he said before licking his lips and roaming his eyes over my body.

I stood there thinking of the way he made me feel. Vice made me feel like the most beautiful woman in the world. When we were together, his sole focus was only on me. Vice gave me his undivided attention. He didn't seem to care about his 2014 Audi that continued to run as we stood on the porch arguing. He paid no mind to the ringing of his phone, nor did he give a damn about the bee that annoyingly flew in his face ever so often.

If this man is making me feel like one of the luckiest women on Earth already, then how will he make me feel as his woman? A lot of females want Vice. Shit, a lot of females done had him. I still don't really know what's going on between ol' girl and him, but whatever the case, it can't be as serious as it seems...right? Look at me, being stupid. The bitch said she was pregnant.

"Aren't you about to be a daddy, nigga?" I asked with my hands on my hips.

"She's not pregnant." I rolled my eyes, and he pulled his phone from his pocket, "Fuck I'ma lie for, Storm? Want me to dial her up?"

"Nah, you good. It's not even that serious."

He scrolled through his phone, and then put it to his ear, "If the possibility of me being a father is what's stopping you from being my lady, then it is that serious."

I couldn't believe he was actually calling the bitch. I stood there waiting, wondering if she did in fact say she's not pregnant, if I'd look for another excuse not to be his girl. I was having a battle in my mind. Shit, I wanted to jump in his arms and tell him *hell yeah I'll be your lady,* but I knew better.

"Jos," said Vice before taking his phone off his ear and putting it on speaker. "What did the lab results from the pregnancy test say?"

"What? Why?"

"Stop playing with me. What did they say?"

"Negative, but I said I want to get a second op—"

He hung up on her in midsentence, then he put his phone back in his pocket and grabbed my hands, "Joslyn is an ex I'm still in the process of getting rid of. Damn, just tell me you'll be mines so we can get the fuck from out here, lil' mama."

I sighed and said, "Alright Vice, but look, like I told you, I don't come second to no female, alright? I'm not jumping into this relationship just to end up being hurt."

He simply stared into my eyes before slowly leaning down and kissing me on the lips, "Damn, a nigga been wanting to do that since I got here." He gripped my hand tighter and started to walk down the stairs. I didn't move.

He looked back at me and said, "I told you, lil' mama, my intentions aren't to hurt you. Like I said, what the fuck I look like going through all of this just to lose you? Come on now."

I nodded, smiled, and let him lead me to his car.

For most of the ride, he spent time on the phone. The shit irritated me. I annoyingly scrolled down Facebook, Instagram, and Twitter the whole time. He'd look my way ever so often or rub my leg, but that was about it. He sat there driving, discussing drug business like I wasn't a total stranger. I mean, it made me uncomfortable but also showed me that he trusted me, or didn't think I was stupid enough to rat on him. Whatever the fucking case, the twenty-minute ride to the damn Crazy Horse was boring.

Wait though, did I happen to mention that The Crazy Horse is a strip club? This nigga was tripping, and when we parked and he finally ended one of his many calls, I let him know.

"A titty bar, Vice?" I shook my head, "The fuck you think this is?"

He looked at me then laughed, "You ever had food from a strip club, lil mama?"

"I've never stepped foot in a titty bar."

He unbuckled his seatbelt, "Well lil mama, get ready to eat the best lamb chops you'll ever taste."

I've heard about how good the food at The Crazy Horse is, but for this nigga to really pull up shocked me. Like I said, Vice just don't give a damn. I'm not a bougie broad, so I unbuckled my seatbelt and hopped out the whip. Some women feel intimidated about their men going to the strip club. Me? I don't care and if invited, I wouldn't mind going with him. Like now. I was just taken aback about why we were here.

Vice met me half way around the car and grabbed my hand. He gripped my hand in a way that said he didn't want to let go. I didn't want him to. I gripped his the same. Although we just met, like I keep saying, I felt a connection with him. Like this was supposed to happen. I'm a firm believer in everything happening for a reason.

We walked in the bar and Dej Loaf's *Me U & Hennessy* blasted through the speakers. For it to be five o'clock in the evening, the bar was a little crowded. There wasn't many dancers working, but the ones that were there was working the floor like a mothafucka. The club was the total opposite of how I envisioned. I thought it would be musky and rundown. Instead, it was quite classy.

Vice was greeted with a hug from a half-naked waitress. Immediately, he introduced me to her as his future wife. She smiled politely and introduced herself as Ginger.

"Vice is a thoroughbred ass nigga; if he likes you, then home girl I love you," said Storm with a reassuring smile; then she nudged me in the shoulder and said, "A lot of these thot bitches in here love him. So don't even trip if they throw shade."

I smirked, "Girl, I couldn't give a fuck less," I giggled, "I'm not one to trip over shade being thrown. I'm good as long as boundaries aren't crossed."

She laughed and told Vice I was feisty. He simply nodded, because as usual he was on the damn phone. I understand he's a busy nigga, but why even invite me out if all he's going to be doing is talking on the phone?

When we finally sat down, he held his finger up, asking me to hold up. I sat there with a frown on my face, arms crossed over my chest. What felt like exactly a minute later, he ended his phone conversation. He leaned over and kissed me on my forehead. Forehead kisses. Man, this nigga exuded sexiness. I couldn't even stay mad at him. I've never been kissed that way. My exes were basic as fuck.

"I apologize about the constant phone talking," said Vice, looking down at his phone again, "But peep, now it's just you and me. Business will just have to wait." He showed it to me, and the screen was black.

I went into my bag and turned my phone off as well. Vice reached over and grabbed my hands.

"Now, I'd like to learn more about the woman I plan to marry," he said with a serious face.

I was baffled. I couldn't really understand his infatuation with me. I mean, I'm feeling him too but damn, the serenity in his voice couldn't be anything but genuine. He made me feel like the luckiest woman on Earth.

A bar full of naked bitches, and his attention is placed directly on me. A bar full of bitches who wants him, frowning up at me, prancing all around our table, but he couldn't care less. A bar full of thirsty bitches who wouldn't stop asking if HE wanted a dance. Not we. They acted as if Vice was the only customer in the place. It wasn't the most crowded, but there were niggas in here that didn't have a chick with them. Still, they flocked around him, but he paid them no attention. And when they asked if he wanted a dance? He told them to get the fuck on with a simple hand gesture, never turning their way. It was like I was the only woman in the room.

"Vice, we just met...why do you be talking like that?"

He licked his lips and shrugged his shoulder, "I trust in myself. My intuition is always accurate. I move off vibes. I only get good vibes from you." He nodded,

"You're a rare type of woman. They don't make 'em like you no more, lil' mama. Why do you think I ain't tryna hear that friend shit? Fuck I look like letting another nigga hit the jackpot?" he laughed, "Hell nah, brown skin, you were made for me."

I blushed, "You crazy boy."

"Just a hood nigga keeping it G with you," replied Vice before picking his menu up.

I smiled as I picked mine up too. Shit might seem strange, us ordering food from a strip club, but when my lamb chops were brought out, I could definitely understand the hype. I couldn't even be cute as I ate. I fucked that food up. Damn near spit a mouth full of food out cracking up at Vice, who made jokes about me scarfing my food down. I couldn't help it. As soon as that juicy meat hit my taste buds, that cute shit went straight out the window. Plus, I felt comfortable enough to be myself around him.

Anyway, I had lamb chops, mashed potatoes with chives, and a Patrón margarita. Vice had the same thing, except he had Hennessey to drink. We stayed in the club for about two hours, and spent the majority of our time getting to know each other.

I learned a lot about him. He was big on trust and keeping it real. I told him that was fine with me, because I did nothing but keep it real. I learned that he had a sister who he hadn't seen since he was a kid. As Vice sat there talking about his upbringing, I couldn't help but notice the sadness in his eyes. He tried to mask it, but I peeped it. The way he rushed his words told me that he didn't like going down memory lane.

On our way out of the club, you wouldn't believe who I actually bumped right into. Branden. He's not my boyfriend or anything like that, but I felt some type of way–not because he was in the titty bar, but because I was out with Vice; mainly because B hit me up last night asking to go out for lunch. I told him no way before I even knew Vice wanted to go out. I told B I was going to call work to try to pick up extra hours. I really had those intentions. Now I just looked like a damn liar.

"Wassup Storm, baby," asked Branden with a smirk on his face.

I nervously smiled and said, "H-hey B," all while avoiding eye contact with Vice, who stood beside me.

"What you doing here?" asked Branden, eyeing Vice up and down.

Is this nigga crazy? He must not have heard about how crazy Vice is. Maybe he did and just didn't give a fuck? Nah, B doesn't strike me as the thug type at all.

I looked over and up at Vice's face and smiled. He wasn't smiling though. His facial expression was stone cold. He gripped my waist, and held me tightly before addressing Branden.

"Wassup, dog? You need something?"

B shrugged and hit on his bottom lip, "I was speaking to the lady."

I intervened, "Um, it's okay Vi—"

"You know it's disrespectful to speak to a woman while she's with a man, right?" asked Vice before letting me go and taking a few steps closer to B, "I'm a man who doesn't tolerate disrespect, my G."

Vice stood there with his hands in the back pockets of his designer jeans, looking down on B, who was about four inches shorter than him. B held his head up and stared at Vice with the same intensity in his eyes. The beef wasn't even about me. I could tell. Vice felt disrespected, and as he said he doesn't tolerate it.

I walked over and stood beside Vice, "Let's go," I said while grabbing his arm.

He was drawing unnecessary attention. All of the stripper bitches were watching what was going on and since we were on our way out, the people coming and going were watching as well. We were standing right at the entrance, so people in traffic could see what was transpiring too. People stood near with their phones out, recording. I heard people whispering *'Aw shit, Vice about to knock this lil nigga out'.* I even heard some women saying I wasn't worth it, sucking their teeth, rolling their eyes; just being straight up haters.

Vice smirked at B before walking away and bumping him in the process. I looked over my shoulder at B and mouthed an apology. B just scrunched his face up at me and proceeded into the bar.

When we got in the car, Vice said, "You can't be entertaining fuck niggas while we're together, Storm."

I put my seatbelt on, "We just got together. I haven't had a chance to tell Branden anything."

Vice started the car and turned my way, "But you did find time to tell him you apologize though," he reached over and rubbed my chin, "Don't ever apologize on my behalf. You have nothing to be apologetic for. As you can see, I don't give a fuck. Neither should you."

I didn't even realize he noticed my little apology. I just shook my head and sat back in my seat.

Us Against Everybody: Miss Candice

[CHAPTER TEN]
JAI

I couldn't believe this nigga was about to make me work. I'm really not tripping, because the job is guaranteed to put some serious racks in my account. Still, I'm a lazy bitch–but I do love to dance.

Percy, my sugar daddy, is part owner of The Crazy Horse, and he talked me into coming down here. I can't stand being around a lot of broads, because I always get hella hate from them. Its gon' be hard for me to work around a bunch of bitches because I pop off quick. Percy told me to leave all of that hood shit at home, but what he don't understand is if some bitch tries me, she'll be handled in the worse way.

Anyway, I was sitting at the bar taking Patrón shots, waiting on Percy to come from the back. It was after nine on a Friday night, and the club was banging. I'm not a shy bitch, but I've never had to get undressed in front of a bunch of people. Thinking about what I was getting myself into caused me to order another shot.

It wasn't like Percy was forcing me to strip. I could've easily walked right out, but I had a point to prove. His old ass told me I was too dependent on him. Said I was too lazy to go out and get it. So here I am. About to get it. I hated when people said I wasn't capable of doing something. I've thought about

117

stripping before. I just didn't think I had to since I had stupid niggas dishing out money. Stripping and gold digging was similar in many ways, so this would be a piece of cake...right?

"Jai baby, you actually came?"

I turned my head and was face to face with Percy. Old ass. He was old enough to be my granddaddy. No lie. But he was a handsome old man. Salt and mainly pepper colored hair, light skin with light brown eyes, and straight teeth that I swear are dentures. He says they're not. Fuck out of here. Anyway, he's about five feet eight, and surprisingly pretty in shape. Don't get the wrong idea; I haven't and will not fuck his old ass. All I do is talk to him. We go out every now and then, and he gives me what I want. A certified sugar daddy.

"Yes I came, what did you expect?"

He sat beside me at the bar and ordered a cognac. Old ass.

"Honestly, I was expecting a text message full of excuses from you," said Percy, sipping from his glass. "You ready, baby girl?"

"Yeah, I think." I looked around the club, "These bitches better not act up."

Percy laughed and shook his head, "You better not act up, Jai. Best behavior."

What he said was going in one ear, and out the other. TUH. If a bitch act up, trust I'ma act a nut.

Even though there were signs that clearly read NO SMOKING, Percy lit a Cuban cigar. He turned my way and said, "Gone in the dressing room if you serious, Barbie."

"Barbie?"

He looked me up and down, then said, "That's what you look like. Barbie. That'll be your stage name."

"I was thinking more like Caramel or some shit. I ain't a blonde, white chick."

Percy stared at me briefly before saying, "Were white Barbie's the only ones made?" I frowned and shook my head, "Alright now."

"But I don't even have my license yet," I said, trying to think of every excuse in the book.

"We'll worry about that tomorrow, Barbie. Stop procrastinating and show me that you ain't a lazy chick."

I tossed my twenty-two inches over my shoulder, finished shot number five, and then made my way to the dressing room. On my way there, a few men tried hollering at me, and some hating bitches turned their noses up. See, this is why I only fuck with Storm. She's my one and only, my BFF for life. She's one female who's never shown an ounce of jealousy, and vice versa. We uplifted each other. Bitches these days don't know the real meaning of friendship.

As soon as I entered the dressing room, I got more stares. I mean shit, I'm not shocked. I'm an intimidating looking broad. I'll easily snatch each and every one of these bitches' customers with no problem. I don't even have to stand on stage and shake my ass. As you can tell, I can get whoever I want. I wasn't even dressed to dance, and on my way here I got approached by over five niggas. Fuck, I can easily walk up on stage and stand there looking pretty. Bet dollars be thrown at me.

I ignored them and walked to the back of the dressing room to get undressed. I didn't want to be around any of them mad ho's.

I opened a locker and started to get undressed.

"You the new booty huh?"

I closed the locker up and was face to face with the prettiest bitch I've seen in here thus far. I mean, she ain't prettier than me, but she sure is badder than the rest of these ho's. She stood at about five feet seven inches with chocolate skin, chink-eyed dark brown eyes, and full lips like Meagan Good, but she favored Gabrielle Union. Her ass was so big you could see it from the front.

"I guess you can say that," I replied, beginning to get dressed in my dancewear.

She extended her hand to me, "I'm Genie."

I shook her hand, "Jai."

"Stage name?"

I rolled my eyes, "Barbie."

She laughed and looked me up and down, "Ain't gon' lie, you do look like a fucking Barbie. Long ass blonde bundles, big ass perky titties, perfect face." She nodded, "Yes bitch that name suites you."

"Excuse me?"

"Girl, don't trip. I meant bitch in a friendly way." She sat down on the bench, "You ever danced before?"

I shook my head no and she continued, "Well it ain't as easy as it looks. You need something to take the edge off?"

I looked at her just as she was snorting a line of coke, "Nah, I'm good. I had some shots."

She laughed, "If you think that liquor is going to loosen you up, you's a fool." She handed me a small bottle full of the powdered substance, and I declined the offer again, "Alright, *Barbie*, I give you two nights. You'll be looking for me and this dope shit."

Genie stood up and said, "Be careful, too. These bitches in here are conniving and envious. If you even seem like a little competition, you'll quickly become the enemy," she said before walking off. I watched her sashay away, long ponytail tickling the top of her ridiculously big ass, with a scowl on my face. Was that some type of subliminal warning? Cokehead bitch.

Once I was dressed, the dressing room was empty. The clock on the wall read 11:00PM. The music was banging; Nicki Minaj's *Boss Ass Bitch* was echoing throughout the club. It was jumping; I knew because I peeked out there a minute ago. A bitch had cold feet.

I stood at the sink, leaning over, looking in the mirror and trying to give myself a pep talk. I wanted to call Storm, but she didn't know what I was up to. I didn't tell her. I didn't think she would judge me – sis never did. But I was a little embarrassed. Crazy right? I'm a proud ass gold digger, but I'm ashamed to tell my BFF I'm stripping. Fuck it. I need to talk to her. I picked my phone up and called her.

"Hey bitch, wassup?" she answered.

"I got something to tell you, but –

Before I could get it out she cut me off, "Aw shit, bitch, you fucking my daddy?"

I burst out laughing, "Sis, stop playing with me!"

She laughed, "What then?"

"I'm at The Crazy Horse."

"Okay? I told you I was just there the other day. So what you in the titty bar—"

I cut her off, "I'm about to dance."

"Whaaaat? Aw shit, bitch why didn't you tell me earlier? I could've came through and made it rain on yo sexy ass!" We both laughed and she said, "What time you going on?"

"Fifteen minutes. I'm nervous, sis."

Storm sucked her teeth, "No need for that. You a bad bitch, you own any room you step foot in. I know this is different but Jai, you the boldest broad I know. Go on that stage and take over sis." She paused, "Damn I wish I could be there. Gone on stage and fuck it up boo."

I cracked up laughing, "Alright, I probably just need another shot."

"Uhn, uhn, take it easy on that. I don't need you up there falling all over the place."

"Oh yeah, you right," I giggled, "Thank you sis, I swear I love yo ass."

"I love you too baby. Call me when you're done counting all them one's up."

We laughed together again, and I heard my name being called. We hung up and I took a deep breath.

[CHAPTER ELEVEN]
VICE

A nigga couldn't even brush his teeth in peace. The phone never stopped ringing for shit. I even put the main line on call restrictions. Only one person had the number to the phone that was ringing now. Reek. The line was to only be used for emergencies.

I spit the Crest toothpaste in the sink and rinsed it out. I let the phone ring as I rinsed my mouth with Listerine. I mean shit, can a nigga take care of his hygiene before work called? For me not to be a hands on nigga like that, I stayed busy. Busier than the dudes that were hands on.

I had just hopped out of the shower and was standing in my bathroom getting dressed. I'd only had about four hours of sleep and was back at it. The life of a hustler. I never slept. I wasn't complaining, because ain't shit ever came to a sleeping nigga but dreams, and I needed more than that. Money was always on a move. Time never stood still, so why should I? I should've been taking better care of myself but shit, fuck it. I can sleep when I retire. I chuckled. I'm never retiring. A nigga ain't leaving the game unless it's in a body bag.

I left the bathroom, walking around my crib ass naked. I didn't give a fuck about the neighbors next door who I constantly caught peeping at me. House full of young bitches I never gave the time of day. I liked teasing them. Liked showing them what they couldn't have. Mothafuckas always calling niggas thirsty, but the thirst be mad real with broads who can't have what they want.

I grabbed the phone from the end table and called Reek back.

"Wassup nigga?" I asked.

"Code 5."

I hung up and sat on the couch, digesting what he just told me. Code 5 meant one of my spots were hit. Code 5 meant one of my biggest spots were hit. The house that brought in the most dough. I was hot. Heated as fuck. I sat there with my fingers intertwined–blood boiling, eye twitching. Today was pick up day. I was about to pick 30K up from that one house alone. 30K of my money in the hands of some bitch made ass cops.

Thirty minutes later, I was dressed and riding down Seven Mile. I was on my way to Reek, who was on the block. Same block the Code 5 house was sitting on. My mood was sour as fuck. I couldn't understand why and how the house got hit. We had cameras all around that bitch. Cameras on the street signs–shit,

127

we had cameras blocks away. That house was my prized possession. I made sure shit was secure, but now for it to be bled dry? Man that shit just didn't sit well with me.

I made a left on Riopelle and slowed up, eyeballing everybody on the block. Some gave me head nods, some shouted a wassup. I didn't say anything to anybody. According to me, everybody was a suspect and when I say everybody, I literally mean everybody.

I parked in front of the Code 5 house that used to be the house I stayed in with my aunt and cousins. Yeah, I turned that bitch into a dope spot. I stared at Reek approaching my whip through the rearview mirror. Nigga maneuvered through the crowded sidewalks slapping hands with niggas, flirting with bitches, like I wasn't sitting here pissed off and waiting on him.

When he got in the whip, he tried to give me a five. I looked at his hand, then up at his face.

"What happened?"

Reek waved me off and said, "Five just came through on some monster shit."

I leaned over against the door, biting on the inside of my jaws, "What happened to the surveillance?"

Reek rubbed his chin, "Shit bro, fuck if I know. You know Darnell and them other young niggas were posted in here."

"Where were you?"

"Kicking back at Jaymo's crib. But I popped in from time to time."

"Who was in the video room?"

Reek shifted in his seat, "I...I don't know bro. I didn't even check."

I chuckled and nodded my head, "Aight, get the fuck out Reek."

"Man, what the fuck you pissed at me for—"

I interrupted him by putting the .45 to his head, "Fuck out of here, nigga! You ain't on yo job! Fuck you mean you was kicking back at Jaymo's? Nigga is Jaymo paying you? Is Jaymo the nigga that'll save yo life if I decide it's time to take it? Sloppy ass nigga! Do you know how much dough this crib was bringing in?! Do you know the type of loss I just took? And you sitting here on chill mode like it's nothing," I laughed, "Maybe you want to die."

Reek was unfazed by the burner to his dome, "Cool off, brodie. You hot right now. Hit my line when you calmed yo hot ass down man." He went for the door handle, "You ain't the only nigga that took a loss, Vice."

He got out, and I sped off.

Was today piss Vice off day or some shit? I had other runs to make, but the news about the Riopelle bust threw me off. I went back to the crib, just to catch Joslyn climbing through my back window. As soon as I saw her skinny legs hanging out of my window, I snatched her ass right back out. When we came eye-to-eye, she looked like she'd seen a ghost. I knew I looked scary. I was pissed off and I liked to kill this bitch.

I pinned her up against the house, "What the fuck you doing breaking in my crib, Jos!?" I yelled in her face.

"I don't have anywhere else to go Vice, damn!"

"Go wherever you been sleeping for the past five nights."

"My car is parked behind the garage, Vice! I've been sleeping there whenever you're home."

I frowned up at her, "Bitch, you been breaking in the crib?"

Then came the tears. Tears I couldn't give a fuck less about.

"Please Vice, I just need another week. Please."

I shook my head, "Fuck no. Stay with yo peoples."

"I can't go back there. You know how humiliating that'll be."

"More humiliating than me catching you breaking in my crib, Jos?"

She lowered her head, "Yes."

Before we became enemies, Jos and I had a strong relationship. She expressed to me how she rebelled against her peoples. She left her happy home to pursue a relationship with a thug they didn't approve of. That was when she was seventeen, and now six years later she's still rebelling. Joslyn ain't been home since.

I walked away from her and closed the window, then proceeded to unlock the door. She followed behind me and I said nothing. I removed my shoes, and then my white tee. I was tired and wanted to take the rest of the day off, despite all of the shit I had to take care of. It was still early; if necessary, I'd handle that shit later.

I took my jeans off and walked around in my Ralph Lauren boxer briefs. Joslyn stood in the kitchen at the sliding doors, looking like a deer caught in headlights. Stupid ass didn't know what to do with

131

herself, and I didn't care. It was only noon and I'd already experienced enough drama for the day.

I walked past her to the refrigerator to pour me a glass of orange juice. I heard her sniffling every now and then, but never turned her way. I wasn't going to give her the attention she was seeking.

I sat at the kitchen island going through mail, sipping from my glass. She slowly approached the island, then took a seat across from me.

"What's stopping you from getting your own shit, Jos?" I asked her without taking my eyes from the bills in front of me.

"I found a condo downtown. I'm short a few hundreds."

"How much?"

"Six."

I stood up and headed to my bedroom. I said before that I look out for women in need. Even though Joslyn gets on my fucking nerves, I can't have her sleeping in the car. I didn't care about her on a relationship level, but we had history. I'd be a mark ass nigga to let her sleep in the car while I'm living comfortably with thousands of dollars.

I shut the door behind me and went for my safe. I entered the code 0823 in the keypad and opened it, exposing neatly stacked hundreds. I grabbed a stack out and locked it back. I sat on my king sized bed and counted the money. Five racks. Over four racks than what she needed, but fuck it. I took a hell of a loss earlier, but fuck it. It's more of where that came from. Joslyn makes an honest living at the hair salon she works at, but sometimes that shit just don't cut it. She's living client to client. I got her. For now. I just need her to get the fuck out of my life, to be honest.

I joined her back in the kitchen and dropped the stack of money on the island in front of her.

"Make it work, Jos," I said before walking off.

"Wait...Vi—Vice, this is too much."

I sat on the couch and turned the TV on, "You welcome shorty. Lock up on your way out."

\-------------------------------------

I couldn't sleep. I'd been tossing in turning in this bed for hours. My mind stayed on that drug raid earlier. I sat up and looked at the time on my phone, ignoring the missed calls and texts. I'd been in bed for two hours, mind racing. I sat on side of the bed and texted Reek.

ME (4:14PM): Meet me at the safe house. Tell them other niggas too.

REEK (4:17PM): Bet.

133

I sat there for a minute, scrolling through my missed calls and noticed Storm hit me up three times today. Damn, lil' mama is my woman now, ain't she? Shit, a nigga done had so much on my plate today that I didn't even think to hit her up period. I felt like shit, but I'll just have to hit her up later. Right now I had some business to take care of.

I left the crib twenty minutes later and headed to the safe house. The safe house is where we went when shit got hot. If I wasn't so pissed off earlier, this would've been my first stop. I thought it was best for me to cool off at the crib first though. Ain't no telling what type of nutty shit I would've been on otherwise.

The safe house is a bullshit ass three-bedroom crib I had my aunt put in her name over on Six Mile and Bloom. Like I said, we only met up there when shit got hot or I needed to lay the law down on forgetful niggas.

I made a right on the block and slowed down, mentally taking notes on the whips parked out front. I told Reek to make sure certain niggas were in attendance. One was missing. Darnell. He should've been the first mothafucka there, seeing as though he was in charge of the spot that got. If I didn't already know no one got knocked, then I'd think the bitch nigga was in lock up, but clearly that wasn't the case.

I parked in the driveway and hopped out. As usual, the young thots yelled wassup and tried to get my attention and as usual, I gave them none. You would think they understood how I got down by now. All I ever did was handle business if I was over here, and anyone who knows me know that I don't fuck around when I'm taking care of business.

I walked in the crib, and the room fell silent. Didn't I express to you earlier how I actually enjoyed walking in on mothafuckas discussing me? I smiled and squeezed into a small spot on the couch between these big niggas named Mook and Pete. I snatched the bag of Flamin' Hot Cheetos Mook was scarfing down away from him and ate a handful.

"Fuck y'all niggas talking about?" I asked with a mouth full of chips.

Mook squirmed, and then Pete's overweight, high cholesterol, diabetes having ass stood up.

I looked up at him, "What's wrong with you, brodie?"

He shook his head, "Too close man."

I waved him off and laughed, "Where the fuck Reek at? And y'all still ain't told a nigga what the convo was about."

I was fucking with them and they knew it. Still, no one had big enough balls to tell me I was the topic of discussion.

"Reek in the backroom with Keesha rat ass," said this short cocky nigga named Benno.

I hopped up from the couch and headed for the room in the back. This house wasn't for fucking with bitches in, and Reek knew that shit already. I swear, bro been on some sloppy shit lately. Earlier he was too busy kicking it with Jaymo and them other dusty ass niggas to keep shit on track at the spot. If he would've been on his P's and Q's, he would've had time to get the drugs and money out the crib.

I pressed my ear against the door and shook my head at the moans from Keesha. Bonafide freak bitch, but a rat to the core. I partook in a little train running on her a few years back. Reek was a part of that shit. Seems like brodie forgot, because it seemed like he was catching feelings.

I opened the door and said, "Keesh, get the fuck up outta my spot thotty."

Immediately, she hopped off Reek's dick and gathered her belongings. She was out the room before she could even put her clothes on. I turned my head and watched her ridiculously phat brown ass wiggle as she hurried out.

Reek sat up on side of the bed, pulling his boxers up, "The fuck bro? I was about to bust a nice one."

I crossed my arms over my chest and said, "You so busy back here getting your dick wet, have you noticed that D ain't in attendance, fool?"

He scratched his dreads and stood up, pulling his joggies up, "Yeah bro. I don't know where that nigga at."

"You send anybody looking for that pussy nigga?" I asked with my face scrunched up.

"I was about to get around to that, V."

I waved him off, "Ahh, shut the fuck up Reek! You been sloppy all fucking day!" I walked out of the room and yelled, "Let's get this shit over before I lose my fucking cool. Matter of fact, Mook, find that bitch nigga D cause if I have to go lurking for him, I might fuck around and kill that dude."

Mook was Darnell's brother, but did I give a fuck? Hell nah, when have I ever? He stood there with a frown on his face, but did he say anything to me? Nah. He scurried out the crib searching for his incompetent ass brother.

The rest of the soldiers in attendance followed me to the dining room, where we sat at a long cedar wood table. I, being the boss, sat at the head, and Reek was on my right; right hand man, on the right of me, but he was pissing me the fuck off. He wasn't up on his right hand duties like usual. He knew I was hot. I was staring at his goofy looking ass.

He chuckled, "What nigga, damn?! I slipped up."

I nodded, "You can think its all fun and games now, my nigga. Fuck around and slip up and come up missing."

Like I was a bluffing nigga or something, he waved me off. Reek did a lot of that, because I've never really put hands on him. I was a loose cannon when it came to other niggas. He peeped that and got comfortable. I liked niggas to be comfortable. Reek my man's and all, but I won't hesitate to snatch the life right up outta his ass.

"Anyway," said Reek, leaning over on the table, "We have to discuss the bust earlier," he said to the other niggas at the table.

I nodded and said, "Travis, since Darnell's weak ass ain't here and you was the only other nigga in charge at that house, where was the nigga that was supposed to be watching the monitors?"

He sucked his teeth, "Nigga was taking a piss br—"

I stood up and walked down to where he was sitting. I looked down on him and said, "He was in the bathroom?"

Travis looked up at me and said, while stammering over his words, "Y-yeah, I know what you said u—"

I rubbed my chin and smiled, "But nothing nigga! I told y'all fuck niggas there were supposed to be eyes on those monitors at all times! I couldn't give a fuck less about a nigga having to piss," I laughed, "Shit, he could've utilized the many pop bottles all around that bitch."

Travis stood up, and I looked at him like he was crazy. He held his hands up and sat back down.

"Look, V, somebody was supposed to sit in while he went bu—"

"But, but, but! Nigga all I'm hearing from you are excuses!"
"Come on now boss," said Trav with his head down.

I rubbed my nose and said, "Its cool, my dude." I extended my hand to him, "Pleasure doing business with you, Trav. Get the fuck up out my spot."

Travis stood up, looking over the table at Reek, who just threw his hands up.

"I can't say shit about Vice's decision, bro. I feel him a hundred percent. The house took a big ass loss."

Trav turned to leave, then turned to me and said, "Somebody talking. Them pigs came through and went right to the stash spots. Didn't even look for us. We were hiding in the walls watching the whole thing. They had an agenda. Didn't give a fuck about a few trap niggas."

He walked off, and I stood there digesting what he said. I stood there looking at everybody in attendance, staring in the eyes of every young nigga at the table. I was searching for the bitch in niggas. The snitch in niggas. I wanted somebody to tense up. I needed somebody to shift in their chair, but no one did, and that told me that the snitch wasn't in attendance. If the niggas in charge of my spots weren't talking, then who was?

Darnell and Mook didn't turn up until the meeting was over. I didn't even feel like smacking the piss out of D, so I just stared at him long and hard. I was looking for the same shit I was looking for earlier. All I seen was fear. I didn't cut him off like I did Trav. Instead, I slapped hands with him and told him I understood why he was trying to stay out of the radar. He was worried about me. Thought I was going to murk his ass. Not now. Not today. I needed him to get comfortable, and when he did that, I was going to pay him a visit. I needed to ease the fear in him so I'd be able to peep the traits of a snitch nigga.

I sat in the car for a minute, looking at the digital clock on my screen. It was damn near nine o'clock, and I hadn't talked to brown skin all day. I knew she was going to be dumb hot at a nigga.

I dialed her up, and she answered with attitude, "Yeah?"

"My bad brown skin, a nigga been busy all—"

"Ummm...who is this?"

I sucked my teeth, "Don't play with me sexy."

"I mean, this can't be my so-called boyfriend? The guy I haven't heard from since yesterday afternoon. I mean, this can't be!" she replied in a playful tone. She was joking, but I knew she was low key pissed about it.

I shook my head, "Let me make it up to you tonight, Storm. I've been busy, lil' mama."

"If you're too busy for a girlfriend, why did you even ask to be with me?" she paused, "Anyway, alright–you can try to make it up to me."

"Try?"

"Yeah, try nigga."

"Trust, a nigga about to make it up to you."

"You're going to have to do something pretty amazing to do that."

I sucked my teeth again, "Fuck you mean, brown skin? I am amazing. It's nothing!"

We laughed together, and just like that I had her.

[CHAPTER TWELVE]
STORM

I hung up the phone and rolled my eyes, with a smile on my face; a smile I tried my damnedest to hold back but damn, that nigga's way with words was crazy. I couldn't stay mad at him for long. I mean, yes I am mad we haven't talked, but I do have to respect the fact that he is a busy man.

I got up from the chaise in my mom's living room and joined her back on the patio. We were having a daughter-mama day, sitting poolside sipping margaritas. My mama was the coolest mama I've ever met, and no I'm not just saying that because she's my ma. I sat next to her as we dipped our feet in the water.

"Who was that that had you run up in the house?" asked my mama, looking at me over her Ray Ban shades.

Immediately I blushed, wishing I hadn't. My parents didn't know about Vice. I wasn't ready to reveal him to them yet, mainly because I was thinking negatively. Like, I didn't want to introduce them and have him end up hurting me. How would I look? I'm not getting any younger, and I keep ending up in failed relationships. No matter how much of a strong bond Vice and I have, I still think of the *what ifs*. Plus, Vice is a dealer. I'm quite sure moms won't approve. Hell, daddy won't neither, and that'd be hella hypocritical of him.

"Nobody."

"Mmhmm, well nobody is obviously somebody special. I've never seen you blush so much. Not even when you were with Nico's worthless ass."

I squirmed at the mention of his name, "I mean...yeah he's special, but not special enough to meet you."

My mama took her feet out of the water and turned her body towards me, "Oh he has to be. Like I said, I've never seen you blush so much." She paused, "What's up? You always tell me about the new boo's in your life. Why are you hiding this one from me?" she rose her perfectly arched eyebrow, "he ugly?"

I cracked up laughing, "Ma! No!" I stared off into space, "He's actually, very very attractive."

"Well hell! Invite him over, Storm."

"Ma..."

"Ma what? Why you tripping?"
"He's a..."

My mama threw her hands up, "drug dealer? Aw hell, Stormy."

"See? Ugh!"

"You're a grown woman, Storm. I can't sit here and tell you who and who not to date. Hell, I'd be a hypocrite it I told you not to. You already know what type of profession your daddy was in, but what I will do is tell you to be careful. Don't make the same mistake I made thinking your daddy would stop for me." She shook her head, "he wouldn't even stop for you. But anyway...those type of men won't stop until they want to. And some never want to. Don't stress yourself out neither. If things start to get too crazy, you know what to do."

I put my hair in a ponytail and lowered myself into the pool, "Relax Mama. We just started kicking it. You talking like we're engaged. Trust, I know what I'm doing, okay?"

She sipped from her glass, "Mmhmm, you sound just like me twenty years ago."

I smirked at her and went under the water. It's not that I wasn't listening to what she was saying. Oh, I was paying attention. I just didn't want to hear it, simply because I knew this would happen once I told her what he did for a living. I could just imagine what my pops was going to say. He wasn't going to tell me to leave him neither. Mack was going to want to know who, and I'm quite sure he knows exactly who Vice is. He knows all of the hustlers before and after his era.

After avoiding the drug dealing boyfriend conversation with my mama, I was finally getting out of the pool. She was in the house on the phone. I swore up and down she was telling my daddy what I just told her. They were divorced, but they still get along very well, like best friends.

I walked in, drying myself off and heard her say, "She just walked in. You want to talk to her?"

She approached me with the phone, and I frowned up and whispered, "You told him?"

My mama gave me a look as to say, 'are you serious?', and I knew she didn't tell him then. I blew her a kiss and took the phone from her.

I smiled, "Hey Daddy."

"What's up princess?"

"Nothing much, I miss you," I said as I took a seat on the couch.

"I miss you too. Come see me at the bar later."
"But...umm...I have a date."

He paused, "Date? Great, bring him with you."

What the fuck was I thinking? I should've told him I had to work or some shit. I rolled my eyes and cursed under my breath. No matter what excuse I tried to throw at him, he wouldn't buy it. I didn't want my daddy to meet Vice yet. I should've known he would want us to come through if I mentioned a date. I wasn't thinking right.

"Um...okay Daddy."

We ended the conversation with 'I love you's, and I got ready to head home.

As usual, I didn't know where we were going. I just decided to wear a long pale pink dress with high slits on both sides. Under the dress, I wore some light blue jean shorts since the slits stopped at my waist. On my feet were a pair of pink low converse. My hair was still laid. I wore it to the side, feathered with loose curls. I was as casual as possible. I just hoped this nigga didn't end up taking me to a high-end restaurant.

I sprayed on some Chanel perfume and like clockwork, he called and told me he was outside. I grabbed my designer bag and headed out of the house. As usual, he met me at the door with roses.

I took them from him and smiled, "You always bring me roses."

Vice winked and kissed me on the lips, "You're special, brown skin. Gotta let you know I peep that in you."

I giggled and went back in to toss the old roses and put the news ones in fresh water. He followed me in. Vice had never been in my spot. I turned around and told him no one invited him in. He looked around and said my place was nice. I thanked him and headed for the front door, but he stood there blocking my way.

"You look beautiful as always, Storm," said Vice, gawking down on me like he wanted to take a bite out.

I nervously fingered through my hair, "Thank you. You look good too, Vice."

He bit his lip and said, "Are you ready to start our date?"

"Yeaaah...about that. Where did you have in mind?"

"Shit, I was thinking about hitting Starters up."

"What a coincidence. My pops is part owner over there and he wants to meet you."

Vice paused, "Damn, already huh? You must be talking good about a nigga."

I laughed, "I haven't even had the chance to mention you to him, for real. He told me to come see him, and I told him I had a date." I shook my head, "That's where I fucked up at."

Vice put his hands in his pockets, "Where you fucked up at? You ashamed of me or something, lil' mama?" I was about to respond, but he smiled and said, "I'm fucking with you, let's roll."

We talked the whole ride to the restaurant. He asked me questions about my pops for the most part. I didn't hold back. When I told him my daddy used to hustle back in the day, he kind of tensed up; then that's where the real questions came up. Thing is, I didn't know shit about what my daddy did for real. Vice asked questions like what hood did he slang in and things like that. I didn't have a clue. All I knew was he sold drugs and Mama left him because of it. Oh, and he eventually went to jail because of it. I think the mention of my daddy being a dealer made him uncomfortable. Hell, it made me uncomfortable too. I really didn't know what to expect.

Twenty minutes later, we were downtown Detroit, on our way to Starters. There wasn't a parking space, so we walked hand in hand the small distance to the restaurant. For this nigga to only hustle over by Seven Mile, people sure knew him everywhere we went. I swear, everybody we passed spoke to him. I almost had to whoop some ass too.

We were almost to the restaurant when we were getting ready to pass a group of females – excuse me, I mean hood rat, thot ass bitches! As soon as they seen Vice, they hurried over to us.

"Hey *stranger*," said one of the bitches eyeing me up and down.

Vice glanced at her and said, "Wassup."

One of her friends chimed in, "What's been up with you nigga? Why haven't you hit my girl up?"

I'm assuming her 'girl' is the tacky bum bitch that called him stranger. Vice didn't say anything to her. He pulled me closer and we kept walking, while these bitches walked with us.

"Damn KiKi, I guess he wifed up now," said another one of her friends while giggling.

"I guess so huh," said KiKi, "It ain't shit, he'll be done with this bitch in a couple weeks and calling me. Ain't that right, Vice?"

Vice stopped. I mean, he stopped dead in his tracks, with no warning. I wasn't really fazed by the jealous bitches. As long as neither of them stupidly put hands on me, I was good. All that tough, slick talking was just that–talking–but Vice was visibly annoyed, and he let them know it.

He turned to me and said, "I apologize, lil' mama." I started to ask why, but he turned to KiKi and her entourage and said, "Get the fuck on. Dirtball ass bitches. I didn't call her because I was done with her." He frowned up and said, "Stop disrespecting before I make y'all ignorant ho's regret even stepping to me."

KiKi's friend started to say something, but she intervened, "Let's just go. If basic is what he likes, then ay!"

"Far from basic sweetie," I smiled.

Vice turned my way and shook his head, "Don't ever, I mean ever, waste your breath on jealous females who aren't even a tad bit close to your level," and then we walked away.

I couldn't even trip. Like I've said so many times, Vice is a very handsome dude. I won't be naïve and think I'm the only woman he's been with. Bitter bitches are to be expected while dealing with a man of his stature. Vice is the type of man any woman would want to hold on to. Look at the lengths Joslyn went. Hell, I just met him not even two months ago, and I don't want to lose him, so I can't act an ass when bitches step out of boundary. I won't give them the satisfaction of my anger. I'll simply smile, just like I did before. It's nothing. I don't see any woman as competition. Why should I? I will do whatever's necessary to keep this man happy.

Before we walked into Starter's, Vice stopped and turned to face me.

"You aight, brown skin?"

"Yeah, I'm good. Why wouldn't I be?"

He nodded, "I hope you understand my apology. I can be a nutty nigga some times, and I'd rather you not see that side of me."

I smiled, "I like all sides of you, Vice. It's cool."

"It's not. I don't want you getting any bad ideas about fucking with a nigga. I can only control myself; I can't control what comes out of the mouths of past broads. I can only try and hope that you peep the serenity in my voice when I say you're the only one I see."

I just kissed him, grabbed his hand, and walked into the bar.

I texted my daddy to let him know we were here, while Vice was conversing with a group of men. He held me close to him the entire time. I smiled sweetly as he introduced me as his wifey. It felt good to be introduced as such, but one of the men made me feel uncomfortable. He kept staring at me and shit. I had to excuse myself to get away from him. Vice didn't give me their names, so I didn't know who the fuck he was. Even if he did tell me their names, I still wouldn't know who the guy was. He was bold as fuck for staring at me like my nigga ain't nutty as hell.

On my way to the restroom, I bumped into my daddy. He gave me a hug and immediately asked me where my 'new boyfriend' was. Daddy was being casual, but I knew he wanted to grill him. That's what he always did when I started a new relationship. He didn't like my ex, and I should've took that as a sign right then and there, but I just figured he was hating like daddy's do. I prayed like fuck he liked Vice, because I was going to be with him regardless.

"You look gorgeous as usual, Stormy," said my daddy, hugging me again.

I smiled, "And you look like you're on a hunt for thotties."

I was telling the truth. Although my daddy was damn near fifty, he didn't look a day over thirty-five. Mack was handsome, and dressed in nothing but designer clothing. He kept up with the trends, and even had a head full of long neat dreadlocks. He's deep brown skin with thick eyebrows, and dark brown doe-shaped eyes with long eyelashes. Let's not get on his body. My daddy swore up and down he was a young cat. He wore a goatee, and I was happy he didn't give in to the 'bearded' trend. When we went out together, people thought we were a couple. Ugh.

"You know me, baby girl," said my daddy with a smile and wink. "Now where he at?"

I pointed across the room, "Right there."

Immediately, he tensed up, "You fucking with Vice?"

"Fucking with?" I frowned, "What's wrong with you? He's my boy—"

"Ex-boyfriend," said my daddy, retrieving his phone from the back pocket of his True Religion jeans, "End that."

I looked at him like he was crazy, "What? Daddy no. I'm a grown wom—"

"A grown woman, but still my daughter. I said end that shit, Storm," he yelled, drawing attention to us.

I looked across the room, hoping Vice didn't see what was going on, but he did. I prayed to God he didn't come over here, but yeap, he did. I liked to run out of there when he walked up to us and extended his hand to my daddy with a smirk. It was obvious that the two of them knew each other and weren't too fond. I just didn't understand it. How could they have beef with each other and they were from two different eras?

"Wassup, Pops?" said Vice.

My daddy looked him and up down, ignoring his extended hand. He looked to me and said, "Get rid of this joker, Storm," and then he walked away.

"What was all of that about," I asked with an attitude.

Vice laughed and bit on his bottom lip, "That's Pops, huh?"

"Yeah, now what the fuck is going on?"

"Dear ol' dad don't like me, brown skin," he said before grabbing my hand, "Let's get the fuck out of here, ma."

I yanked away, "Nah, obviously some real shit is going on. I need to know why he don't like you, Vice!"

He stared at me long, and hard before replying, "I'd rather not talk about it here."

Just as I was opening my mouth to say something, my daddy and two other big burly guys approached us. They told Vice he had to leave. I was stuck. I didn't know who to go with. My loyalty lies with my daddy because he's my daddy, but damn, I'm feeling Vice and I feel like something is definitely wrong. I felt confused. Vice though, was unbothered.

He smiled and winked at me, "I'll hit you up later, lil' mama. Don't worry 'bout none of this."

My daddy stood in front of me and said to Vice, "Get yo young reckless ass up outta here boy. You won't be hitting her up," then he turned to me, "Aight that right, princess?"

I just shook my head and watched them escort Vice out of the bar. I walked off in the direction of my daddy's office. Just as expected, he was following behind me. When we made it to his office, he slammed the door shut.

"Do you know what type of nigga you dealing with, Storm?" he yelled in my face.

I was caught off guard. My daddy never yelled at me. He always treated me like his princess. In his eyes, I could do no wrong. I was hurt so like a big baby, so I cried.

"What?! What is the fucking problem?"

He pointed his finger in my face, then walked around his desk and took a seat, "you gon' watch your mouth for one, Storm. You might be grown but let's not forget who the parent is here." He slammed his fist down on his cherry oak desk, "Damn! How long you been fucking with that boy?"

"What is the problem daddy!? Seriously."

He rubbed his goatee, "Vice killed Lando."

I wanted to say *'tell me something I don't already know'*, but I just stood there with my arms crossed over my chest. Lando wasn't anything to us for real. I mean, sure we grew up in the same hood and what not, but it's not like we considered him family. He wasn't to us what Jai is, so I really can't understand the problem.

"Okay, what's that got to do with us?"

My daddy chewed on his bottom lip and shook his head, "Don't say one word to your mama…"

"About what?"

"Lando and them other niggas worked for me. I was his connect."

[CHAPTER THIRTEEN]
VICE

Storm was in the middle of some serious shit. It killed a nigga when I peeped who her pops was. I couldn't stand that nigga, and the feelings were mutual. He was Lando's connect. The nigga who purposely had Lando set up shop on my blocks. He was a ballzy ass old head, but he wasn't a threat for real. Mack stayed out the way, but something was telling me that he was going to do the exact opposite of that once he finds out I'm fucking his little girl. What? I might not be balls deep in them guts now, but I will be. Storm ain't leaving a nigga alone. She's smitten.

I sat behind the wheel of my Audi in front of Reek's crib. Yeah, I was pissed at him earlier, but this was the norm for us. I'd get pissed, talk my shit, and put the burner on him; he'd tell me to cool off, I'd do that, and we'd eventually link up like nothing happened. Reek is the only nigga that understands me. Well, besides my cuzzo Dawson. We've been rocking for a minute now. I met the short nigga when I was sleeping in the shelter. As soon as Rico put me on, I put Reek on. I saw something in him. The loyalty was obvious.

Like I said, I met Reek at the shelter. I was a new nigga, hating it. Brodie seemed hella comfortable in them fucked up ass conditions, mainly because he had been staying there for almost a month. Anyway, I was pissed and refused to lay on them dirty ass mattresses. Reek peeped the disgust in me, and he offered me some disinfectant wipes and clean linen. Since then, I've considered him family.

He hopped in the whip, and we slapped hands.

"What's the word, brodie?"

I looked at him with a smirk, "You ain't gon' believe who brown skin's pops is."

"Who?" asked Reek, firing up a spliff.

I laughed, "Mack."

He looked at me and said, "Fuck you laughing for then nigga?"

I shrugged, "Fuck that nigga. Bitch nigga liked to bust a blood vessel when he peeped I was his son-in-law."

We laughed and Reek said, "You know how that nigga got down back in the day though, right?"

"Back in the day, bro. Back in the day." I pulled off, "I'm the grim reaper now, my nigga." I took the blunt from him and pulled from it, "The mothafucking grim reaper. And them sharing blood won't stop me from snatching the life away from his ass if need be." I slapped hands with Reek again, "It's nothing, my nigga."

I was dead ass serious. I cared about Storm, but let's be honest. If a nigga is gunning for me, then I'm gunning for him. Fuck who he's affiliated with. I'm the type of cat that'll put a hot one in Mack's dome, comfort his daughter at the funeral, and eat fried chicken at the repass. I just didn't give a fuck, which is why I'm on my way back to Starter's right now. Most niggas want to impress Pops-in-law. Obviously, I ain't most niggas, right? I thought we'd already established that.

I passed the blunt back to Reek and told him to pass me the Bvlgari shades out of the glove box. He was reluctant because it was dark as fuck outside.

I looked at him and said, "Nigga, pass me the fucking shades."

He handed them to me, and I put them on and did sixty the rest of the ride to Starter's.

I parked a few businesses down and sat there for a second. I decided that it was only right to text Storm before I rolled up in there on some nutty shit.

ME (9:12PM): WYA

STORM (9:12PM): Still up here, why?

ME (9:13PM): Yo old man still there?

STORM (9:13PM): Just left. We need to talk.

I sat my phone in the cup holder and punched the steering wheel. Reek turned to me and asked what was up.

"Bitch nigga left."

Reek put the blunt tail out and looked at me, "Yo, what the fuck was you gon' do anyway?"

I smiled, "Shit bro, you know me. I just wanted to taunt him a lil' bit," I winked, "Wanted to see how mad I could get 'em. You know old heads be trippin when it comes to their daughters."

Reek laughed, "You a petty ass nigga, dog."

I shrugged, "I just like seeing how much I can piss a nigga off. Tempt 'em a little bit. See if their tough enough to pull the burner out."

"You gotta stop fucking around like that though, bro. Niggas getting killed out here every day, Brodie."

"Stop talking to me like I'm not responsible for the high murder rate out here. Fuck, nigga I know what's what."

Reek was always rapping to me like that. Thing is, I just didn't give a fuck. If a nigga's stupid enough to pull the heater out on me and not pull the trigger, then that man must be ready to die. It was like playing Russian roulette out to this mothafucka. Living in the D is like that. You never know when your time is coming, which is why I live my life to the fullest.

I grabbed my phone from the cup holder and called Storm.

"Wassup," she answered, sounding annoyed.

"You mad at me or something, lil mama?"

"Nah, what's up though? I'm trying to get me an Uber."

"Fuck out of here with that mess," I said, "Don't insult me like that, brown skin."

"I'm not trying to insult you Vice, but my daddy did have my ride thrown out."

I bit my tongue. Literally. The bitter taste of blood hit my taste buds, and I hated the shit. I almost showed Storm a side of me I didn't want her on the receiving end of. Her pops did have me escorted out, but I didn't need her reminding me of that shit. To relive that disrespect made a nigga's blood boil.

"Yo, I'm outside."

"What? Please don't come in here."

I shook my head, "Brown skin, baby..." I bit my tongue again, "A nigga's not rolling up in there. I'm here because I knew you'd need a ride home," I said, lying through my teeth.

Reek sat beside me laughing his ass off, and I had to stop myself from doing the same. Shorty just didn't know what type of cat she was really dealing with. Jai should've told her. She should've warned her about how off the chain I can get. In a way, I'm glad she didn't wire her up with too much information. The last thing I wanted to do was scare lil' mama.

"Okay. I'm outside, where you at?"

I snatched my shades off and hopped out the whip, heading in her direction. I told her I was coming. The phone was silent for the most part. Lil' mama was feeling some type of way. She let her bitch made pops get in her head. *It's nothing a night of long dicking won't fix,* I laughed to myself. Man, I'm not a shady dude with ill intentions. I'm just a man, falling for a pretty brown-skinned sista. Of course, I'd like to bend her over, play with that monkey, and enter her from behind. What nigga with a dick wouldn't want that?

We met each other half way. She didn't know what do to with herself. I could tell. She was stuck, so I helped her out. I hung the phone up and pulled her into my arms. For a second there she tensed up, but the tighter I held her, the more she let go. Shorty was mines, and there was nothing Mack could do about it at that point.

After I dropped Reek back off at the crib, I headed for Storm's crib. She was silent. Too quiet for somebody who claimed we needed to talk. I glanced at her from time to time. She rested her head on the window, with her eyes closed. I shook my head and turned my attention back to the rode.

Earlier, I told her I didn't need anything giving her regrets about fucking with me. I could see the regret on her face, and that shit pissed me off. I could tell she was confused. I could tell she was fighting with herself, trying to decide if she should stay or leave.

I looked at her again, and she was bobbing her head to Dej Loaf and Future's track *Hey There.*

> *I still taste you on my lips, yeah I do*
> *Last night we made love 'til the Sun came*
> *I know it's hard when I leave, I'm not with you*
> *But when I'm gone, hold it down, you're my love thing*
> *You be doin' it, that one and two, that four thing"*
> *Let's slow it down a bit, I'll hit you with that foreplay*
> *Hop on top, I start to ride you, that's that horseplay*

Strip for my baby, bitch we ballin', that's that sports play...

I turned the stereo down, "Storm?"

"Shhh, this my shit," she said before turning it back up.

I turned it back down, "I thought you wanted to talk."

She looked at me and playfully smacked my hand away from the knob, "And we will when we get to my crib." She turned it back up, and I shrugged.

When Future's verse came on, I turned it down again and said, "Fuck the Earth, it's us against everybody. Right?"

She looked at me with a smirk, "What you trying to get me to say, nigga?"
I laughed, "Ay lil' mama. Whatever you feel."

She nodded, "Yeah, Vice, it's us against everybody."

I smiled and did fifty the rest of the way to her crib.

When I pulled out front, she took her seatbelt off. I sat there with the engine running. I didn't know if shorty wanted me to come in or what. She still hadn't said much to me, and I'd be damned if I act like a thirsty ass eager beaver just to get in the crib. That's not even my style.

She looked over her shoulder at me and asked, "You coming, ugly?"

I laughed while confidently licking my lips and rubbing my chin, "Fuck out of here lil' mama, you know a nigga fine as hell."

We both laughed and I turned the engine off, unbuckled my seatbelt, and hopped out the whip. She stood there gripping her bag with a silly smile on her face. When I made it around the car, I grabbed her hand like her front door wasn't a few feet away. I just wanted to touch lil' mama. Her small soft hand fit perfectly in my big rough ones.

"Yeah you fine. Sitting there fronting like you don't want to kick it in my house," she said with a smirk.

"Brown skin, a nigga ain't pressed about kicking it in yo lil' crib. Chill," I replied with a smile, "Besides, it ain't like I'm about to get deep in them guts," I smirked, "You wanna rap about the petty ass beef yo pops got with me."

She playfully punched me in the arm, "Oh my God. I swear, you don't care about what you say." She put the key in the lock, then looked at me over her shoulder, "And nigga, you won't be getting deep in these guts for a couple months. Fall back, thirsty McThirst."

I licked my lips and looked at her perfectly shaped ass, "I was going to hit you with a slick ass comeback, but I can't get over how fuckin corny that thirsty McThirst shit was."

She opened the door and we walked in, cracking up. Lil' mama was so down to earth. I hope she ain't really tripping over that shit with her weak ass pops.

I kicked my Nike's off and plopped down on her couch. She looked at me with a scrunched up look, and I threw my hands up.

"Can a nigga make himself at home, brown skin?"

She giggled and kicked her shoes off, then joined me on the couch. Storm put her hair behind her ear and looked back at me. So fucking beautiful, yo. I wanted to pull her down on top of me. Fuck what she wanted to talk about. Vice didn't want to talk. Vice wanted to get balls deep in them walls, but lil' mama wanted to act all 'morally'. Lil' Mama can talk that couple months shit all day. If I put hands on her in the right way, she'll be throwing that thing back tonight; but I had to be a gentleman.

"On some real shit, we do need to talk about what happened earlier, Vice," she said in all seriousness, while looking me in my eyes.

I nodded and sat up so that'd we be side to side, "Aight lil' mama. What's up?"

"You know my daddy?"

"I know of him. Fuck ni—my bad...he use to slang back in the day. Now he just slang from a distance."

She nodded, "I know. He mentioned how you killed Lando."

I shrugged, "That a problem?"

What? You thought I was about to sit here and deny taking that man out? Fuck no. You should know by now. I gives no fucks. If she felt some type of way about me spilling his blood, I couldn't care less. I could tell she really didn't care. She seemed a little bothered, but not enough to stop fucking with a nigga. That there showed me that she was a thorough chick. A thorough chick I needed on my team for sure.

She drew her lips in her mouth, then said, "Um...you really just don't give a fuck huh?"

"Am I supposed to?"

She stared at me briefly before saying, "Should I be worried?"

"About what?"

"This beef you got with my daddy. It seems like you're a ticking time bomb with no remorse. Should I be worried about shit escalating between you two?"

I sat there a moment. I couldn't tell Storm the first thing that came to mind. Which was *'if anybody should be worried, it should be Mack'*. I couldn't scare her like that. I couldn't come off so strong. I couldn't tell her that I would off his old ass without a thought. I couldn't tell her I'd split his melon right in front of her if ever necessary. Nah, I couldn't tell lil' mama that.

So instead, I said, "You don't need to be worried about anything," without adding too much emphases on you. I pulled her closer to me and said, "Shit's cool ma. As long as Mack stays in his lane, I'll stay in mine."

I should've shut up. There was absolutely no need to add that last little line in there. As soon as the words left my mouth, she tensed up and pulled away from me.

"What that shit supposed to mean, nigga?"

I sighed and pulled her into my chest again, "Ahhh, come on now, brown skin. Let a nigga live. I'm not trying to sit up all night talking about the petty beef yo pops got with ME."

Mack never liked me. That's why he put Lando and his crew on in the first place. He told them bitch niggas to post up on my blocks. He knew I would act a donkey. Mack didn't like me because he said I was an arrogant nigga. Said I didn't know shit about hustling. Fuck he talking about? I'm getting cake out here. If it wasn't for Rico putting that dope and them good ass greens in my hands, then niggas in the D would still be smoking bammer ass weed, and the fiends would still be dropping like flies. I kept the good shit. I hustled the good shit. I supplied these streets. Not Mack's old ass. His time was over in the nineties.

Bitch had ill feelings. Mad because I was pulling in more bread than he could even think about back in the day. Nigga hated me so much that he came out of retirement just to put Lando on. He thought Lando could fuck with me. How stupid of him. Pop's reeeeeal mad now. I put his nigga in a casket. Mack thought it'd go the other way around. Nigga clearly didn't know much about Vice. Not as much as he thought he did. Fuck nigga–I am death.

She shook her head, "This shit is so fucked up."

I looked down her shirt and said, "Ain't it though, lil' mama?"

She mushed me in the head and adjusted her top, "Ugh, thirsty ass."

172

I laughed and said, "Can you blame me? Hell yeah a nigga thirsty, and you looking like an ice cold glass of water, lil mama."

"Stop playing so much Vice, real shit's going on right now."

I shook my head, "You think real shit going on because this is new news to you. Mack been hating a nigga. He just hate me more now that I'm son-in-law and shit," I laughed, and she rolled her eyes. "On some one hundred shit Storm, stop stressing. Do I look worried?" I asked, pointing my thumbs back at my chest.

"That's because you arrogant and just don't give a fuck."

"Right. So be easy, brown skin. Be easy." I licked my lips and said, "And let a nigga put hands on you, girl."

Storm started to say something, but there was a knock at her door. More like banging. I knew who it was. She did too. Mack was here. Good thing I kept the banger on my hip.

Us Against Everybody: Miss Candice

[CHAPTER FOURTEEN]
JAI

Storm kept calling me, but I was busy. I was settling perfectly at The Crazy Horse. This was night three, and my clientele was slowly but surely climbing, honey! I wasn't even nervous anymore.

I snorted a line of the potent white stuff and threw my head back. I hated to admit it, but Genie was right. I needed something to take the edge off to do this shit. Working here was optional, but I liked the money it got me. I didn't have to fuck niggas – if I didn't want to – for it neither. I was making my own money. I wasn't waiting on a nigga to do for me. It felt good. So yeah, I'm dancing. That's what I want to do now. My first night alone, I made about about eight hundred dollars. Do the math, bitch. If I wanted to dance for a full week that's roughly a little under six thousand fucking dollars. Just to get on stage and shake my ass. Sure, I had to dish out a little towards payout, but that's nothing!

It's not like I'm a damn crack head. I just snort coke from time to time. Only a little when I'm here and trust, it's the good shit. Genie's dope man is official as fuck. As a matter of fact, she gets the shit from a dealer that works for Vice, and everything that nigga sells is top of the line.

I stood at my locker getting ready to dance. I put my bikini top on and said, "Tie this up for me, Genie."

I fucks with Genie on some official shit. She rubbed me wrong when we met, but she's cool as hell. Not to mention, the bitch has a crush on me. A big one at that. Genie is known in the club as a boss ass bitch. She's head honcho, and everybody knows it, so I need her on my good side. I've been finessing the fuck out her, and I don't even swing that way.

She stood up and grabbed the bikini top strings, grazing my nipples in the process. I didn't say shit, but I did cringe in disgust. Genie knew I didn't fuck with bitches, but she kept trying me. I didn't stop her though. I even agreed to put on a show last night.

It was crazy as hell, and the coke had me lifted. Us doing a show together was spontaneous as fuck. Well, for me it was. When I hit Genie up about snorting a few lines, we got high and right after, she asked me to put on a show for the customers. I was down. I knew it'd get me a lot of cash and new clientele. I couldn't back down. Besides, the drugs had me on another level.

Everything was cool until I noticed Ryan in the crowd. Unlike the other niggas in attendance, he wore a frown on his face. I was caught red-handed. He didn't know I was stripping. Why would I tell him that? But obviously, someone had told him otherwise so yeah, we locked eyes just as Genie was pretending to go down on me. I didn't even stop her. The coke had me gone and instead of reacting like I usually would, I smiled and winked at him.

I thought shit was good, because after Genie and I finished our little act, I couldn't find him. I didn't run into Ryan until after the night was over, when I was walking out of the club hand-in-hand with some corny nigga who had just thrown serious cash at me. By then though, my high was diminishing, and I came to my senses once I saw Ryan standing there. He was pissed, and I was embarrassed. I didn't want people knowing I was dancing, but who the fuck am I kidding? I shake my ass at one of the most popular bars in the D.

Anyway, once he noticed me leaving the club with a guy, he walked off, and bitch I ran right after that meal ticket. What the fuck you think? This nigga got serious cash lined up. I couldn't give a fuck less about a nickel and dime hustling nigga that threw one's at me. I was trying to seal the deal on a sent future. Fuck you thought? Ryan is a damn good college football player with offers lined up!

When I finally caught up to him, he wanted nothing to do with me, but I'm a bad bitch—and very persuasive, might I add! I batted my eyelashes, stroked his ego, and even played on his flaws. Yeah, he's still got them same ass bumps on his face that I don't mind rubbing on to pretend I care.

He basically told me to stop dancing, but fuck that. I'm here, high, and ready to make some bread. What he don't know won't hurt him! He lives all the way in Ann Arbor; but shit, somebody still snitched on me. I was playing it careful though, and decided to cut my schedule down to three days a week. I'll still bring in serious cash, so it's nothing.

"Mmmhm, they fucking," I heard one of the dancers whisper.

I knew she was talking about me and Genie. People been talking since last night. I couldn't believe that I've only been working here for less than a week and I already had problems.

"Nah Cinnamon, no the fuck we ain't," I replied, walking towards the vanity next to the one she was sitting at. "And if we were, it ain't none of you bitches' business."

Genie walked up and stood behind me, just as I took a seat. She ran her fingers through my hair and said, "Stop lying, Barbie. You always worried about what a mothafucka got to say." She leaned down and kissed me on the neck, "It's okay boo. Tell them."

I jumped up and said, "Gennnie...stop playing girrrrl. Aint a daaaaamn thing to tell."

By then, the coke was coming in to effect, and my words were dragging. I looked over at Cinnamon and Bunz, and they were giggling. I wanted to smack the fuck out of Genie for confirming some bullshit ass rumor. She knew them bitches were just going to run with that and spread more lies.

178

Genie said, "Bitch, it ain't nothing to be ashamed of. I use to lick Cinnamon a few weeks back." She winked, "Her ass just jealous."

Before I could respond, Genie and Bunz left the dressing room.

I sat down and laid my head on the vanity facing Cinnamon, who was shaking her head.

"You's a weak minded ass female," she applied a coat of MAC lipstick, "You just started dancing here and already Genie done got you." She stood up, "Somebody should've told you to stay the fuck away from that crazy, delusional bitch."

I stood up and adjusted my silk booty shorts, "Aw shut up ho, you just mad she ain't fucking with you no more."

"No more? Tuh! Genie ain't never put her lips on me, stupid. And according to you, five minutes ago, she hadn't fucked with you neither." She shook her head and opened the door, "Be careful. You've befriended the devil. Coke snorting bitch now, crack head in a few months."

After she walked out, I stood there repeating her last words in my head. *Coke snorting bitch now, crack head in a few months...*

Us Against Everybody: Miss Candice

[CHAPTER FIFTEEN]
STORM

I'm a grown ass woman, but I'm hiding from my daddy. He won't leave, and Vice keeps trying to open the door. I wish all of this shit would stop. My daddy ain't letting up though! He keeps banging on the door, yelling my name, and calling my phone. He know Vice is in here. I was ashamed of the way I was acting, but I shouldn't have to choose. What type of shit is this?

I don't see any reason as to why I shouldn't fuck with Vice. What? Because he has some type of beef with my daddy? So got damn what! That petty shit don't have anything to do with me and quite frankly, I think it's messed up that my daddy is making it my problem. Trying to make me choose between him and my boyfriend is nothing but pettiness. I guess he can't stomach the fact that his little girl is in a relationship with someone he despises.

People might think I'm stupid for not getting rid of Vice, but I look at situations from all angles. True, Vice did kill Lando but again, what the fuck does that have to do with Storm? Not a got damn thing. Vice has been nothing but nice to me, a perfect gentleman. I have no legit reason concerning me to break up with me. My daddy is just going to have to understand that.

"Storm! Open this fucking door," yelled my daddy, causing me to jump.

Vice looked at me with wrinkled eyebrows, "Fuck you jumping for?"

"My daddy's never been this mad at me," I said just as my phone began to ring. "Ahhhh! I just need this shit to stop."

"Give me your phone."

I looked at him like he was crazy, "What? Nigga no! Do you not know who my daddy is? Have you not heard the stories?"

Vice bit his lip and sighed deeply, "Look brown skin, I'm not trying to hear all that." He walked closer to me and held his hand out, "Let me holla at him. You not answering him ain't gon' make the nigga go away, love."

I laughed, "The last person he—"

Before I could finish my sentence, Vice had snatched my phone away from me and answered it. I went after him for it, but he dodged me by turning and running away. Once he opened his mouth to speak, I said fuck it.

"Wassup Pops," he answered.
I rolled my eyes. He was only doing this shit to be petty. I could tell by the look on his face. This is not how I wanted things to go with my boyfriend and my daddy. For a change, I just wanted to find someone

he'd approve of, someone he would give blessings to marry me. Shit, he didn't even want me associating with Vice.

Vice looked out the blinds as he talked to my dad, "Look man, banging on the door ain't doing shit but making matters worse. Aight cool, you don't want your daughter fucking with a nigga, but what you have to understand is that Storm is a grown ass woman, my guy."

He was making shit worse; not my daddy and quite frankly, he was being disrespectful. I stood next to him, and then quickly snatched the phone. My daddy was yelling all types of threats to who he thought was Vice. I'd never heard my daddy talk like that. His tone of voice and everything was straight gangsta.

I looked into Vice's eyes as I said to my daddy, "Go home, Daddy. He's about to leave too. We'll talk about this tomorrow, it's late."

"Damn right it's late, so what the fuck that bitch nigga doing here, Storm?!"

"Daddy...just go."

Vice was pacing the floor, biting on his lips. He was pissed. They were pissed. I couldn't choose, so I wouldn't. I'll just cut the both of them off. This shit ain't about to stress me out. Fuck that. Sure, Mack is

183

my daddy but trust, his ass can be cut off too. I can't get over how he's been talking to me. Straight up disrespectful.

I hung up and tossed my phone on the couch. I stood there watching Vice pace for a little while before he finally stood before me.

His eyes burned with anger. I quickly glanced out of the window and noticed my daddy pulling off. Shit. The way this nigga was looking at me made me regret sending him away. I looked past him and at my phone on the couch.

"I'm about to go?" asked Vice, his eyes softening a little.

I took a step back and said, "Umm, yeah. I can't deal with this shit. There's no pleasing y'all."

He stuffed his hands in his pockets and said, "I'm not making you choose, brown skin. I'd never make a bi—I mean, woman choose between me and her pops. What type of nigga do you think I am?"

"The type of nigga my daddy don't want me dealing with," I sighed and ran my hands through my hair. "Look, no offense or anything aight? I'm just...I'm not about to let what y'all going through stress me out. Shit, I'm just going to cut both of y'all off."
He took a step towards me, and I stepped backwards. He kept coming at me, and I didn't have

any more room to back up. My back was literally against the wall.

"You cutting me off?" Vice asked, gawking down on me.

I placed my hands on his chest, and said, "Yeah, it's time for you to go."

He looked at my hand on him and said, "You feel that shit?"

"What?"

"The way my heart is racing."

I nodded and moved my hand, but he grabbed it and placed it back there. His race was beating fast, fast and hard like it was going to explode–like mine was doing the other day.

"You can't cut me off, lil' mama," he shook his head, "Nah, fuck nah you can't. I'm feeling you way too much to let another nigga win. Fuck you mean you cutting me off? Just so another nigga can slide through and reap the benefits? Nah ma, I told you. You were made for me. Brown skin, you're the balance a hood nigga like me need."

I sighed and looked away as my eyes became misty. Things were moving fast. Way too fast. I knew what he meant. I felt the same way. I've never felt this way about anybody–not this soon anyway. We just met two months ago, and he already had me in my feelings–but I couldn't do this. How in the hell is this going to work with my daddy hating him? And if daddy ain't feeling him, then my momma ain't gon' feel him neither.

His phone starting to ring, but he ignored it. Vice grabbed my chin and turned me to face him. I tried my damnedest to stop the tears from falling, but when my eyes met his, I couldn't stop it.

With his thumb, he wiped my tears away and said, "Don't cry, lil' mama." He shook his head, "Yo, if it's stressing you out that much, then I'll let you go, aight?"

I said, "I just have to sort some shit out with my daddy."

He nodded and backed away, "Aight, cool." He laughed, "I can't believe I was just on some sucka ass begging shit. It's cool, lil' mama. Hit my line when you grow up a lil' mo, aight?"

I was offended, "Wait! What?!"

Vice stood at the front door putting his shoes back on, "I spoke well enough for you to understand exactly what I said." He paused, "I went through a lot to get you shorty, but what I won't do is beg you not to leave me. For a change, a nigga was trying to build. I've never wanted to build with anybody. I saw something different in you, lil' mama. Maybe I was just captivated by your modelesque beauty." He laughed, "I'm bugging on some soft shit, but fuck it, thugs need love too." He turned the doorknob and said, "Aight brown skin, stay up."

Before I could stop him from walking out, he was slamming the door closed. I stood at the window watching him walk to his car. Why am I so emotional over this shit? I just met the nigga, but in that small amount of time, I learned a lot about him. In that short period of time, I grew close to him. I fell for him, for sure. I knew that when tears poured from my eyes once he pulled off.

It had been three days since I talked to Vice. As usual, I woke up checking my phone, looking for a good morning text that I never got. I sighed and sat up, staring at a red cardinal sitting on my back deck. Once again, I was lonely and there was no one to blame but my daddy.

Speaking of Mack, I was supposed to meet up with him on my lunch break. Apparently, he had been too busy to meet up beforehand. He was avoiding me because although I'm his daughter, I'm about to cut right into him. My parents were getting on my nerves. Yes, my momma too.

The only person who understood me was Jai. I was actually shocked because my mom and I could always see eye-to-eye, but she didn't give a damn about how I felt for Vice. She was siding with my daddy all the way. Currently, I wasn't speaking to her neither. I'm a grown ass woman – why won't they let me live?

I got out of bed and walked over to the sliding glass doors that led to my back deck. The cardinal was sitting right in front of the door. I swear, he was looking at me. I kneeled down and tapped on the glass, and he flew away. I should've gotten a picture of it to post on Instagram. I stood straight up and stretched before sliding the doors open and stepping out.

It was early in the morning, so the sun was just beginning to peek above the horizon. I stood there, feeling the warmth against my skin, wishing I could go to Miami with Jai this weekend, but instead I had to work. I sighed and walked back into the house before anyone seen me standing there in my bra and panties.

My phone rung and I hurried to answer it, hoping it was *you-know-who*, but it wasn't. It was my supervisor, Carla.

"Hey," I answered.

"Good morning, boo. Grab some donuts before you get here."

"Any preferences?"

"Nope. Oh, and would you mind picking me up a coffee? You won't belieeeeve the night I had. I slept in the parking lot, girl."

"Aw hell naw," I giggled, "I can't wait to hear what had you doing that."

We hung up, and I sluggishly went to the bathroom to shower.

An hour later, I was parking at Tim Horton's. I grabbed my Michael Kors messenger bag and phone from the passenger seat before heading inside. As expected, the place was crowded. I looked at the time on my phone and decided it was best if I called Carla to let her know I'd be late.

"It's crowded girl, I'm going to be about twenty minutes late."

"Oh you straight, just don't forget my Café Mocha." I laughed and we hung up.

"Wassup stranger." I turned around and was greeted by B. I hadn't talked to him since the incident at The Crazy Horse.

"Um, hey, wassup B."

We moved up in line, and I tried to avoid conversation with him. I couldn't tell if he was still upset or what. I didn't look at him long enough to tell if his smile was devious or straight genuine. Honestly, I didn't give a fuck. Running into him here was weird, and I couldn't wait to get away from him.

"What you been up to?" he asked, moving up and standing next to me.

I turned to him and said, "Nothing really. You?"

"Shit, making moves."

"Ohhh, that's wassup."

I was confused. Where was this conversation heading, and why did he think I gave a fuck about him making moves? Like I said, I hadn't talked to him since The Crazy Horse, and that was damn near a month ago.

"You still with ol' dude?"

I laughed, "Naw, Branden, I'm not with ol' dude. Where we getting at?"

"Like I said, I've been making moves. Every hood I try to set up shop at is ran by him—"

"I don't know a damn thing about what you're talking about."

What the fuck? Is this nigga FEDs or something? Coming at me about what Vice does for a living. Did he expect me to put it all on the table? I know nothing about what Vice does for real anyway.

B laughed and said, "Stop acting like I'm the FEDs or something, beauty. I'm just creating conversation."

"About nothing I want to talk about."

He licked his lips and stepped in my face, "Well beautiful, I have missed you. Can we talk about that?"

I told him to hit my line later just to get him the hell away from me. Luckily, I was next in line and he was after me. I ordered the donuts and two Café Mochas for Carla and me, and got the fuck out of dodge with the quickness. I was probably speeding out of the parking lot before B was finishing up his order.

Work was a drag, and I was dreading lunchtime. I really didn't want to talk to my daddy, but it was necessary. I looked at the clock on the wall, *11:43AM.* Lunch was in fifteen minutes and if I know my daddy, he was here already. Just as I expected, he was approaching my counter with a smile and a teddy bear. A damn teddy bear like I'm five years old or

191

something. I half way smiled at him as he stood on the side as I cashed out a customer.

I handed the customer her change and receipt, "Thank you. Have a great day."

My politeness was forced. I wasn't in the best mood. As much as I hated to admit it, I missed Vice terribly. I'm saying that like it's not obvious. I checked my phone every fifteen minutes. Now I have to have lunch with the man responsible for breaking us up. I'm a grown ass woman! Why won't my daddy butt out?

Daddy stood in front of my counter flashing an apologetic smile, and he handed me the teddy bear.

I looked at it and sat it on a shelf under the register, "Umm. Yeah, thanks Daddy."

"You still got that collection, right? I figured you could add to it."

"Those bears are in storage Daddy, I'm not a child anymore," I sternly replied.
He uncomfortably cleared his throat and leaned on the counter, "Yeah, I guess I'm just having a hard time accepting that."

"Mmhmm, well my lunch isn't until 12—"

"Hey Mack! You can go now, Storm girl," said Carla out of nowhere, lustfully staring at my daddy.

I turned around and smirked at her. She smiled and rose her eyebrows at me. I shook my head, grabbed my purse from up under the register, and told her I'd be back. She told my daddy it was really nice seeing him, with much emphasis on *really*. I looked over my shoulder and mouthed 'ho' to her. She laughed and began to ring another customer up.

My daddy draped his arm over my shoulder and asked, "You still mad at me, huh?"

I turned towards him and said, "Disappointed would best describe what I'm feeling. Anyway, we can eat at P.F. Changs."

The rest of the walk to P.F Changs was spent with him talking. He was trying to explain his reasoning. I wasn't really trying to hear it. Again, whatever beef him and Vice had didn't involve me.

I ordered the Kung Pao Chicken, and he ordered the Sesame Seed Chicken. Before I took a bite of my food, I took a sip of my Coke and was ready to address the issue.

"Stop," I said, cutting him off from yet another excuse. "What you and Vice have going on has absolutely nothing to do with me. For you to blatantly tell me to stop seeing him was wrong. And the way you spoke to me? *'Fuck nigga', 'fucking with him'*...what was that about? I can't believe you spoke

193

to me like I wasn't even your daughter. That hurt me more than anything."

He reached over the table and grabbed hold of my hands, "Stormy, baby, I apologize. Seeing you with him just....just upset me to the max, alright? I can't stomach that shi—I mean I can't stomach you being in a relationship with a nigga like that."

"But it's okay for me to have a daddy that's really no different, right? You said you're back in the drug game," I snorted, "Tuh. Look at the pot calling the kettle black."

He stared at me briefly before saying, "You've really grown up on me, huh?"

I shrugged, pulled my hand away, and dug in my food, "Yes, I have. And I'd appreciate it if you treated me like an adult, Daddy."

"Alright Storm, I hear you." He paused, "But I still forbid you from seeing him."

"You can't forbid me from anything. Besides, we're not together anyone." He began to speak, but I cut him off, "And don't think you've won because I'm cutting you off too, Mack. You don't respect me as an adult."

"Storm, who the fuck you think you're talking to? You can't cut me off; I'm your daddy."

I frowned, "Exactly. But I'm not your 'child'. I'm a grown woman. You embarrassed me! I really like Vice, and being away from him is killing me."

He mumbled, "And being around him will fuck around and kill you too."

I rose my eyebrow, "What?"

My daddy slammed his fists on the table, "Fucking with him will get you killed out here, Storm! I can't have my princ—daughter in the middle of this shit! You sitting there on your high horse like I'm trying to keep you away from him out of spite. People hate Vice! And will do anything to get under his skin. You ain't fucking with him because if something happens to you behind his shit...man...the D gon' see a side of me that I buried a long time ago."

Now it made sense. He was protecting me. But I didn't need protecting. I can handle myself–or at least I thought I could. I knew messing with a man like Vice was dangerous, but I couldn't help but be drawn to him. I missed him. I wanted him. I needed him. My days weren't the same without him. Something was missing, and it was him. I'm not sure if my yearning for him was clouding my better judgment or what. I heard everything my daddy was saying and agreed with him. But still, I wanted Vice. Despite it all.

Us Against Everybody: Miss Candice

[CHAPTER SEVENTEEN]
VICE

I reclined my seat and unbuckled my Gucci belt buckle. She smiled seductively and leaned over, fumbling with the button on my True's.

"What you gon' do with that mothafucka, girl?" I asked, looking down at her as she went in my boxers and pulled my dick out.

I was fucking with this lil' bitch I met yesterday. Shorty was a straight up ho, and I treated her as such. We were in the drive-thru line at McDonald's and she was about to dome me up. I figured I'd test her freak since the line was long as fuck and just as I expected, she was willing to go to work on me.

"Damn," she said, gawking at my dick in awe.

"Yeah, ma, I get that a lot." I grabbed the back of her head, "Now put your mouth on it before this line start to move."

She smirked and licked her lips before she slowly took my dick in, inch by inch. I held a fist full of her expensive weave and pushed my dick to the back of her throat. She gagged, and I told her to open her mouth wider. Bitch couldn't suck dick to save her life. I was wasting my time on this lil' ho.

She opened her mouth, and I slammed her head up and down on my dick. She was gagging, and spit was all over my dick and her mouth. When she told me to stop, I snatched her head away from me and pulled my shorts back up.

"I thought you knew what to do with it," I said as I sat my seat back up and pulled the car up a little.

She wiped her mouth with the back of her hand and said, "Nigga you a savage. You can't be fucking my face like that, what's wrong with you?!"

I glanced at her and laughed, "Nah, what's wrong with you? Type of bitch dome a nigga up on the first date?"

She rolled her eyes and touched the door handle, "I was feeling you. That's why. But just lose my number."

I pulled my phone from my pocket and scrolled through a few text messages I missed, "I didn't even lock you in, my baby. Don't even remember your name."

She opened the door and said, "Something is really wrong with you."

I looked up at her and said, "You just might be right. You might want to take them ridiculous ass heels off ma. You got a long walk ahead of you."

She got out and slammed the door. I laughed. I couldn't give a fuck less about a slut bitch. I didn't have time to care about feelings. I had other shit on my mind. Too much on my plate. I should've been out taking care of business, but instead I was fucking with her. A nigga needed some head. I needed to bust a good one. I could've easily hit Jos up. She would've did the job right – no problem. But I wasn't trying to fuck with her like that anymore.

I texted Reek back and told him I'd be around the way in fifteen. He wanted to move in on this one problem after midnight, but I wanted the shit done pronto. I was sick and tired of niggas not respecting the boss in me. It's cool; I have no problem reminded these nigga that's I'm not to be fucked with.

Mack mad as fuck, eh? Got his little minions shooting my spots up and shit. As a matter of fact, he had one hit the night I was at his daughter's house. Salty ass old nigga. It's cool though. I will knock each and every one of them boys off. Yeah, and then I'll go see him. Fuck nigga think I'm unaware of where he's resting his head. Nothing is off limits to Vice. If I need info, I gets info.

I pulled up at the pick-up window, paid, and grabbed my food. The broad at the window kept flirtatiously smiling at me, but what the fuck am I'm going to do with a chick that works at McDonalds? Absolutely nothing. Except get my dick sucked and fuck. I'm sweet on that though. These broads aren't

199

even good for that apparently. I sat the food in the passenger seat, and ate a few fries from the bag before hopping on the freeway.

Fifteen minutes later I was speeding down Seven Mile, blasting *I'm the Plug* by Future and Drake. As always, I was meeting Reek on Riopelle. The house was back open, despite his suggestion not to. That house brought in serious dough, no way in fuck I was about to close up shop for good. I waited like a week and opened back up. It'd only been opened for three days, and the money was already crazily accumulating.

Niggas looking for the plug,
Nigga I'm the plug, really.
Really I'm the plug,
Really I'm the plug,
Really I'm the plug...

I parked the Challenger a few houses down and hopped out. I nodded at a few niggas, and said wassup to a couple females before heading down to the spot. When I stepped foot on the porch, a bad feeling came over me and I went for my burner, then turned around. I stepped down a few steps and looked from one end of the block to the other.

A black old school Monte with tints was coming down the block. I tapped on the front door four times before jogging down the steps. I stood on the sidewalk, burner in hand, eyes on the car approaching. The windows slowly rolled down, and I cocked the burner back. I heard the front door of the house open, and knew off rip my nigga was right behind me. Of course, them other niggas was posted too, but only one I could count on was Reek. Just as I expected, he ran down the stairs and stood right beside me.

"Fuck is that?" he asked above a whisper.

"I don't know yet bro. We about to find out though."

The car sped up, and that's when the shots rang off.

BLOCKA, BLOCKA, BOOM, BOOM! BLAH BLAH, BLAH!

We went running after the car, emptying clips. Everybody on the block ran and hid for cover. Kids were screaming, crying as their parents hurriedly pulled them to the ground. I wasn't concerned about anybody's life but my own at that point though.

"Ah fuck!!"

I looked to my right, and Reek fell to the ground. My nigga was hit. I gritted my teeth and sent a shot through the back window. The car swerved a few times before hitting a tree. I looked down at Reek as his shirt quickly filled with blood.

"Ay! Get bro to the hospital!" I yelled to Darnell, who was running my way with six other nigga behind him.

I leaned down next to him, grabbed his burner, and told him he'd be aight; then I stood up and went for the car smoking up the block. I peeped the driver door open and ran towards them. I lifted the burner and aimed it at his dome, waiting for him to try to run off. I lowered the gun and thought it'd be better if I shot at his legs instead of his head, just to slow him down. I didn't want to murk him from a distance. I wanted to stare into his eyes as I blew his brains out.

"Oh my God!" yelled everybody on the block. They were running towards Reek. I looked over my shoulder at his lifeless body, and my heart sank. Damn, I hope bro straight. I couldn't worry about that right now though. I had me some sucka ass niggas to murk.

The driver was injured. He barely got out of the car before he collapsed. I slowed up as I got to the car. I looked down at the driver, and he was leaking from his neck.

I pointed the gun in his face, "Nigga, are you stupid or stupid as fuck?"

He spit blood in my face, "Ni-nigga fuck you!"

I wiped my face with the back of my hand before sending bullets through his face, ripping it open in an instant. Fuck nigga. I kicked him away from the car and peeked inside at the lifeless bodies. Three other niggas were with him, and none of them looked familiar. If these weren't Lando's niggas, then who the fuck were they?

Two hours later, I was at the crib. I should've been at the 'spital with Reek, but it was hot as fuck up there. I needed to stay the fuck out the way. Hook wanted me too bad. Reek was doing aight. Bro was hit in his chest and in surgery. Darnell hit my line an hour ago. Told me the hospital was flooded with cops. Told me to lay low because they were asking questions, tying everything to me and my organization. I knew it was only a matter of time before they came knocking.

I sat in the living room, smoking a fat ass blunt, hands trembling. Not out of nervousness, but out of rage. I didn't know who the fuck was gunning for me. Those niggas weren't from the hood. Looked like some straight up west side cats. I didn't fuck around on the west, so who?

Funny how life works. I was about to ride down on Lando's niggas the same way I just got rode down on. Slowed me down quick as fuck.

My phone rung. *Jos.*

I answered, "Wassup? You tryna come through?"

"Huh? Hey...where that come from?"

"My dick."

She sucked her teeth, "Vice..."

"Vice what?"

"I'll be there in twenty minutes."

"Good."

I hung up and sat back on the couch. No matter what, Joslyn was always down to suck and fuck a nigga. No matter what we went through, she was always there. She knew I was using her, but she didn't care. Bitch liked it. One thing's for certain though, I was strapping jimmy on extra tight.

I'm only fucking with Joslyn because I'm bored with nothing else to do. Shit, a nigga wouldn't mind kicking back with Storm, but the situation with that is already known. I'm tired of trying to keep a woman who don't want to be kept. If she wanna listen to her pops, then cool–deuces shorty. Despite how I feel about her, begging and pleading for a broad is not how I get down.

Twenty minutes later, Joslyn was knocking at the door. I greeted her with a bottle of Hennessey. Joslyn turned the fuck up off Henn, so it's only right for me to get her wasted off some. She gave me a hug, and I hugged her back. Baby was looking good as fuck too. I've always been into brown-skinned women, but Joslyn's a red bone to the core. Thick in all the right places, although she does have a little gut, but it doesn't take away from her sex appeal. Big brown eyes, full ass lips. If she wasn't a bitch and so whiney most of the time, she'd be wifey material but right now, I couldn't give a fuck less about her flaws; I was trying to get my dick wet, and that's something she's a pro at.

"You must be mad at your little girlfriend," said Joslyn as we sat on the couch. She smirked, "I knew you'd come running back."

"Jos, shut the fuck up with that shit. You already know what it is," I unbuckled my jeans, "Instead of running yo mouth, put it to work."

I would've come off rude to anyone else, but Joslyn loved that bossy shit.

She flirtatiously smiled and sat what looked like her overnight bag on the coffee table, "Can I at least get a drink first?"

I didn't respond. I was too busy focused on the overnight bag. Bitch wasn't staying over here. I intended on letting her know as soon as I busted my nut. I should've known better, inviting her over here.

She talking cash shit, feeling like she won but nah—when it comes to Storm, Joslyn will always lose.

She took three shots of Henny back to back, before she undressed and kneeled down in front of me. Joslyn made direct eye contact as she lowered my shorts and pulled my dick out. Just looking at her damn near made me bust a nut. She had the seductive look down to a science. I might not like Joslyn as my girl, but she's perfect as a fuck buddy.

Joslyn grabbed hold of my dick, and slowly stroked me using two hands. I threw my head back and closed my eyes, anticipating the warm wet feeling of her mouth. Joslyn had one of the best mouthpieces.

She softly licked it before slowly entering me in her mouth. Her lips had a vice grip hold on me. I grabbed the back of her head as she went up and down. My dick was thickly coated with saliva as she deep throated me.

"I love this dick even when it's not inside of me," said Joslyn, staring at my dick in awe as she licked the sides.

"If you love it, stop playing with it baby," I said as I grabbed her jaw and put my dick in her mouth.

She looked up at me and deep throated it, while cupping my balls, licking them at the same time. I grabbed her head and said, "Yeah, like that Jos. Go to work, ma."

BOOM! BOOM! CRASH!

"Put your hands up!"

My eyes shot open, and I pushed Jos off me. Damn, a nigga couldn't even get head in peace.

I stood up, dick standing at attention, and put my hands up. Detective Olivia Thompson stood in front of me and told me to pull my shorts up. I smirked at her and asked if she really wanted me to conceal my weapon. She didn't find my corny ass joke funny, and threw me to the floor, where I laid beside Joslyn, who was crying.

"Chill with them soft ass tears, Jos. They ain't locking yo ass up."

"But what about you?" she asked.

"Don't worry bout...ahhh! Fuck," I yelled out as my arms were forcefully being pinned behind my back.

Dt. Thompson hated me. When she was assigned to my case, I thought having her on my ass would be a walk in the park. Thought having a broad on my back would be easier. I was wrong. Thompson hated me for reasons other than being a suspected dope dealer and murder. She called me a womanizing asshole on many occasions, so obviously she hated me because of that too.

"I didn't see a warrant! While y'all in my crib fucking shit up," I yelled as I was being handcuffed.

They were raiding my house. I smiled every time they left a room empty handed. Fuck boys weren't going to find anything. How stupid did they think I was?

Dt. Thompson shoved a warrant in my face and said, "You're needed downtown for questioning regarding the multiple homicides on Riopelle street as well."

"Baby, I don't know what the fuck you talking about. I've been here posted all day with home girl."
Dt. Thompson kneeled down and smirked, "I'm not your baby. And I don't give a shit about what bullshit story she might have to tell. I know for a fact you were there. I have witnesses spotting you there." She eyed me up and down, "I told you I'd get you, Vice." She winked and stood back up.

Bitch was lying. Ain't a soul on this Earth dumb enough to place me at a murder scene. Niggas might be stupid enough to rap about that drug shit, but murder is a different story. Uptight, stuck up, no dick getting bitch was trying to fuck with my head. Thing is, she couldn't.

"Yeah whateva, bitch. Just get this shit over and if I'm not under arrest, take these fuck ass handcuffs off me."

I could talk to the cops anyway I wanted to. She hated it. She hated me. Bitch didn't like being disrespected. Normally, I wouldn't talk to a woman like this, but Dt. Thompson ain't a woman. She's exactly what I called her; a bitch. A black bitch with a hard-on for incriminating black men. So what I'm not innocent? Why not be a black queen and treat a black king with the respect you're supposed to treat 'em with? The only reason I'm disrespecting her is because the bitch disrespects me every chance she gets.

Dt. Thompson's partner, Detective Charles Henson, forcefully turned me over and yanked me up by my collar.

"Fuck around and stretch my Versace out, you gon' be paying for it pussy," I said with a frown.

He grabbed me again, this time stretching the collar of my shirt out completely, "Whadda say to me, you piece of shit?"

Charles Henson is what I like to call a house nigga. Black dude that uses the word nigger like his own ancestors weren't enslaved by that same word. He hates black men so much that I swear he hates

209

himself. Charles is the type of cat that'll bleach his skin. Now that I think about it, he is a little lighter.

I smiled, "It's cool, my mans. You must be bought pissed as fuck that you've been protecting and serving for years and still can't afford a cold ass Versace shirt."

"The place is clean," yelled a cop coming from the back of my house.

Charles stood in my face, gawking at me. Eyebrows knitted, lips pressed tightly together. He was pissed off. I always pissed them off. They knew I was guilty, but without the evidence what they knew didn't matter.

I kept a smile on my face, "Uncuff me, house nigga," I looked down at Joslyn, "And uncuff her t—"

Before I could finish my sentence, Charles had grabbed hold of me and pinned me up against the wall. He pushed my face into the wall and spat as he yelled in my ear.

"Keep talking! You can be cocky all you want, but listen here, nigger." He grabbed the back of my head and applied more force, "We finally have someone willing to talk. Yeah, your days are numbered, you black piece of shit."

"Man un-cuff me and take me downtown for questioning, dog. I couldn't give a fuck less about the threats you barking out."

I said it before, the law wanted me bad, and whenever they couldn't find anything incriminating, they got emotional.

I didn't get in bed until seven the next morning. After being at the station for two hours, they let me go. I would've been out of there sooner if they wouldn't have been bullshitting on letting me call my lawyer. As soon as he came through, they let me go. I answered a few questions before he got there, just so I wouldn't look suspicious, but when dude came through he was like 'is he guilty of anything?' 'do you have any evidence against my client' 'alright cool, let's go Vice'. Nigga was real official. I knew Thompson was lying about somebody placing me on the scene. The only reason they wanted to question me was because my affiliation with Reek.

Anyway, after I left the station, I circled the hood. I even drove through Lando's block. Wasn't shit popping off over there, which I found weird. Them niggas stayed posted. They knew I was coming for them. That's why they were in hiding.

Now I'm at the crib, contemplating. Phone in my hand, staring at brown skin's name. I miss lil' mama fa sho. Thing is though, is she missing a nigga too? Shorty ain't hit my line period. Maybe she's being stubborn like me. If that's the case, we just don't be talking. I'm not budging.

I sat my phone on the charger and it rang. I picked it up, *Storm*. Ironic as fuck, huh? That's why I say she was made for me. We were thinking about each other at the same damn time, but she hung up before I could pick up.

I sat up and called her back. She answered on the second ring.

"My bad, that was a mistake," she quickly said.

I laughed, "Aight, lil' mama. Stay up."

She just wanted to hear a nigga's voice. Lying ass.

[CHAPTER EIGHTEEN]
JAI

I needed to get high. I've smoked a fat ass cush blunt and I still couldn't get the feeling coke gave me, so I'm riding around the hood looking for Vice. I could've easily ran up in one of his spots, but I didn't want my business out like that. I mean, it ain't like a bitch on crack. Coke is a rich man's drug bitch, so don't judge me!

Anyway, like I was saying, I'm riding trying to find Vice, which could be a waste of time. That nigga didn't touch work, but what was my other option? I called Genie's ho ass, but she's been on some flake shit for weeks now. I guess she's feeling some type of way because I was slowly but surely becoming a favorite at The Crazy Horse. Since the day before yesterday, she's been holding out on the coke; trying to throw me off my game, and I'd be lying if I said it wasn't working.

So now, I need my own supplier. I just need to cop it from Vice directly. I trust him because unlike other niggas in the hood, he ain't with that gossiping shit. This is something I'm trying to take to my grave. I tell Storm everything, and I'm not even telling her this shit.

I stopped at the gas station he goes to the most, and posted up. I grabbed my phone from my MK bag and rolled my eyes. I had two missed calls from Ryan. I can't talk to him like this. Not while I'm fiening for a pick me up. I thought I'd be able to control the urge. I thought I'd only need it at work. I thought wrong as fuck. Fiening for a line was taking a toll on me. I was a snappy bitch when I needed it.

I texted him.

ME: (2:34PM) Hey baby. I'm not feeling too well. I'll HYU later, ok?

I didn't want to deal with anybody. Storm hit me up earlier too, about a dinner date. I haven't even replied. One person I didn't want to be flakey towards was her, so instead of writing a snappy, bullshit reply, I didn't respond. I will after I get this dust up in my system though. I mean, I literally needed the shit. My body was responding badly to not having it. In addition to the irritability, I'd been fatigued all day.

I impatiently looked around the gas station for Vice's car. Nothing. This nigga always came up here. I knew he was in the hood...I saw him circling the block earlier. Where the fuck was he?! I turned my attention back to my phone, staring at Storm's name. I was tempted to call and ask her for his number despite how crazy that'd make me look. Bitch, I'm fiening!

I didn't have to, though. I heard Vice before I saw him. He was getting out of his whip, yelling wassup to a group of niggas. For some strange reason, I immediately checked my appearance in the mirror. I brushed my hair and applied a coat of lipstick. I was about to approach this nigga about some work. Risky as fuck. I didn't want to look as bad as I was fiening.

I hopped out the car and cursed myself for the way I was dressed. I wasn't dressed, actually. As soon as I realized the Cush wasn't giving me the type of high I was seeking to acquire, I left looking for him. I have on a pair of pajama shorts, and a raggedy old t-shirt.

"Shit, bitch you look cray," I mumbled to myself as I approached Vice, who was holding the gas station door open for a group of hood rats.

He held it open for me too; thing is, I wasn't going in.

"Wassup Vice," I said as I self-consciously ran my fingers through my bundles.

He eyed me up and down, "Sup Jai?"

I stood there for a second, unmoving, not speaking.

"You going in or what, girl? Got a nigga holding the door and shit," said Vice, clearly annoyed.

"Nah, I umm...I need to talk to you about something."

Again, he eyed me up and down, this time with a confused facial expression, "Bout what?"

I looked around, "Can't talk out here."

"Aight, wait on me in the whip. I gotta grab a few swishers," said Vice before walking past me and into the store.

I walked away and got back into my car to wait on him. I was shaking like a leaf on a tree. I wasn't worried about him running his mouth in the hood, but I was worried about him telling Storm. What the fuck am I talking about? They don't even talk anymore. But still... who's to say they won't start back? I proudly walk around fucking and sucking...dancing for money...but I cannot have my best friend knowing I snort coke. If I'm so ashamed, I shouldn't be doing it right? Well, habits don't work like that. I knew right from wrong but hell, I didn't give a damn.

When I noticed him coming out of the gas station, I moved my purse and junk off the passenger seat. From the outside, you couldn't tell my pretty pink Benz was as junky as it is. I had shit everywhere.

I was throwing stuff to the backseat when he opened the door. He sat down despite the junk under his feet. Vice sat there breaking his swisher down, saying nothing. The car was quiet for about two minutes before he finally looked at me.

"Fuck you want girl? I've been sitting here a minute and you ain't said nothing."

I nervously giggled, "I was waiting on you to say something."

"For what? You told me you wanted to talk."

Again, I was silent. I was nervous.

"What Jai? You need some coke, don't you," he asked with a frown on his face.

I was alarmed and mad as hell, "What?"

He licked the blunt paper, and I couldn't help but notice how moist his mouth was.

"Don't act so surprised, baby girl. I fucks around heavy at The Crazy Horse. I know what goes down up there." He paused, "Well shorty, you can't come at me for something I don't have. Hit the house on Riopelle, you already know what's up."

I was embarrassed, "Who told you?"

He looked at me, "The Crazy Horse told me, Jai. Like I said baby girl, you know I don't carry that shit on me. If you want it, you gon' have to go get it yourself."

"Vice, I can't walk up in no spot. I can't be seen walking in that house," I said while shaking my head.

He turned and grabbed the door handle, "Why not? Ain't like it's a secret. The streets talk." He opened the door, "Take care of yourself Jai, aight?"

"Wait! You not gon' tell Storm, right?"

He sighed. The mention of Storm changed his demeanor. His shoulders slumped over, and I swear I noticed a sadness in his eyes I've never seen before.

"Jai, I haven't talked to lil' mama in over a month," he paused, "Just be easy on that shit, aight? Coke is an expensive habit. Most mothafuckas end up not being able to afford it and turn to crack. Don't end up like most mothafuckas, aight?" he said before getting out.

I didn't say anything. I sat there crying my eyes out. I have to shake this habit. I already have a rep for being a gold digger – which I don't give a fuck about, but I can't be known as a cokehead. I cannot.

Us Against Everybody: Miss Candice

[CHAPTER NINETEEN]
STORM

I need to grow up. I wanted nothing more than to talk to him, but I couldn't bring myself to call for real. I hadn't heard his voice in so long, and it was driving me crazy. Who would've known? I only knew him for a short period of time, but it felt like something was missing out of my life now that we weren't together.

"Girl, call his ass! I swear when I saw him the other day he looked sad as fuck," said Jai, sitting across from me eating a bowl of Ramen noodles.

"Why you keep saying that, Jai? If the nigga gave a fuck, he would've been hit me up," I said, rolling my eyes before tossing my phone on the couch across the room. I needed that phone far away from me before I fucked around and called him blocked.

"Vice ain't the type of nigga to bend over backwards for a bitch. I can't believe he went through what he did to fuck with you," she shook her head. "Girl, you stupid. Sorry boo, but you are. You know how many bitches out there checking for him? And he had eyes only for you? Tuh! I wish I would let my daddy – rest his soul – stop me from seeing someone."

"It's not even that, for real."

"Uh huh, what is it then, Storm?" asked Carla, coming from the kitchen with her noodles.

We were all kicking it at my house, getting ready to meet Ryan, B, and another one of their cousins in downtown Royal Oak for drinks and hookah.

"I ain't trying to get caught up in his shit if some nigga come gunning for him," I replied. "Too many people hate him."

"Sound like Mack talking to me," said Jai before eating a big fork full of noodles, "Vice is a stand up dude. He wouldn't put you in danger, sis."

"That nigga ain't psychic! Shit can pop off anytime, anywhere," I replied.

Carla nodded in agreement, "I feel you boo. Vice can't protect you from what he don't see coming."

Jai frowned up and said, "Carla, shut up. Storm, you gon' fuck around and be single for the rest of your life thinking like that and listening to her ass. She don't even know Vice! That nigga's official as fuck. He gotta sixth sense or some shit. People say he knew that drive-by was going to happen before the car even rolled up the block!"

Jai's rude as fuck. She's jealous of the friendship I've formed with Carla. For so long, it was just Jai and me but when I started working at Neiman's, Carla and me got cool as hell. It took me a while to even get them to meet and even after that, it took time to get them to go out with me together. It's petty, but that's just Jai. I won't lie and say I wouldn't be on the same tip if she showed up with some new friend. We're protective and territorial when it comes to each other.

Carla laughed, "You seem infatuated, Jai. You sure you don't want him?"

Jai jumped up, "Oh no, sweetie. Don't eveeeen go there. Storm, get your friend before I check her ass boo."

I laughed, "Ugh, keep calm. She's just fucking with you, Jai. You so uptight. What's wrong? You been snappy all day."

Jai sat down and finger combed her hair. "I'm just saying. Carla...you tried it." She pointed her fork at her, "Don't try me again, honey."

We all cracked up laughing. I noticed how Jai's laugh was forced on, off bat. Something was up with her, and I made a mental note to talk to her about it tomorrow.

As usual, we were riding in Jai's pink Benz on our way to downtown Royal Oak, MI. I wore a smile and cracked jokes every now and then, but on the real, I did not want to go out with B.

He was feeling himself on some dope boy shit since he'd started slanging a little drugs here and there. Every time we went out, he made it his priority to flex. Okay, you making a couple coins, that's wassup, but be humble nigga. The way he was acting told me he wasn't used to making the amount of money he was making now, and I'm sure it's not even that much. Like he told me the other day, he couldn't set up on the six or seven, and those hoods generated the most clientele. He was slanging in HP.

Anyway, even though I didn't want to go out with him, I was on my bad bitch shit. I just got my twenty-two inches of Mink Brazilian body wave hair installed with a closure, and I even got my makeup done, in addition to getting a mani and pedi. All day, me and my girls had been together. It was a nice night out. The temps dropped from 90 this afternoon to 83 tonight. Perfect night to dress sexy.

I wore a burgundy body-con dressed that stopped a couple inches above my knees, with a pair of nude So Kate Loubi's with a four and a half inch heel. I was dressed a little dressy to just be going out for hookah, but I wanted to be fine! Plus, I wanted to grab the attention of a real man. B's cool but trust me, if a man (who doesn't look to be a damn drug dealer) steps to me, I'm passing him my digits. It's time I start looking elsewhere. Apparently, Vice couldn't care less about us getting back together. I'm too fine to be sitting up sulking about what could've been.

After Jai paid the parking attendant, we parked and sat in the car a minute, touching our lipstick up. On my lips, I wore Sin by MAC. I'm not a big fan of matte lipstick, but Tia, the girl who did my makeup, suggested it.

"They there already. Ryan said they got a liter of 1800," said Jai with a smirk. "You drinking sis?"

I nodded and finger combed my hair, "Yeah, but you be easy on that shit."

Jai waved me off, "Girl I'm grown."

"Grown and driving."

"If need be, you can push the whip. You're a better drunk designated driver than me, bitch," said Jai, laughing as she looked in the mirror and brushed her hair.

"I just know this cousin of theirs better not be on no bum shit," said Carla, fixing her box braids that were up in a big bun.

Jai looked over her shoulder at Carla, "Nigga might be ugly, but I guarantee he ain't broke."

"What? He ugly?" yelled Carla, "Aw shit, I'm not fucking with him!"

Jai laughed, "I never met him." She shook her head, "You and Storm better get over looks. Money is green, with dead ass presidents on it. That's the only thing that should matter when it comes to a nigga."

I didn't say anything. I was too busy texting Branden back. He was rapping about how he couldn't wait to see me. Earlier he sent me an invite from Glide Video Messaging after I told him I was leaving the shop. He wanted to see me. I installed the app, but didn't video message him. I told him he'd just have to wait. Now he was eager with anticipation.

Branden is a sweetheart, and maybe I'd appreciate that more if I wasn't so into someone else. *Someone else being you-know-who.* I often wondered if I wasn't so captivated by the swag of Vice, if I'd still think Branden was lame.

"Catch me rolling through the city
Riding with the top off
Man my whip so big when you in it
Fuck around and get lost
Told my bitch to let her hair down
What the shit cost
Tell me baby if you bout that life right now
I hope it ain't talk no...
I can put you in the mile high club, what's up?
Let's take a trip.

Have you ever read 'the world is yours' on a blimp?"

When we walked into Hookah Joe's, J. Cole and Jeremih's new hit *Planes* was playing. The bar was packed as usual, but it took us no time to locate Branden and his boys. They had a certain aura about them. They were draped in designer. Everything about them said they had money. B was the flyest, which is a rarity since Ryan always stands out. Since B had been climbing the 'drug dealing ladder', his swag has been on a million–when it came to how he dressed, at least. Personality wise, when it came to spitting game at me, he was still the same–corny and thirsty.

The guys stood to greet us. Jai hugged Ryan, who lifted her off her feet. Branden hugged and gave me a kiss on the cheek. Carla and Pierre, Branden and Ryan's cousin, shook hands. Carla looked pleased. Pierre was a joy to look at, and he was dressed nice. She looked at me and smirked with a head nod.

We took a seat, and I started off with the grape-flavored hookah. I was having a great time; plenty of laughs and liquor. Shot number three had me chill as hell. Branden was in my ear talking about all types of freaky shit. I would've found him out of line if I wasn't tipsy. I would've cut into his ass, but I sat there smiling, puffing from the hookah.

"I'm saying though, can I spend the night, ma?" asked B, rubbing on my thigh.

I might be drunk, but I'm not that fucking drunk. I grabbed his hand and sat it back in his lap. I turned to him and said, "No Branden, you cannot take advantage of me tonight." I giggled, "Okay? Chill."

He smiled and bit down on his bottom lip, "You won't call it taking advantage when you throwing that ass back. You look good as fuck tonight, might I add."

I ignored him. I barely heard what he was saying. My attention was focused on the sexy ass, caramel-colored, hazel eyed, six-foot, boss type nigga sitting across the room. His focus was on me as well, but he was unmoving. Maybe because he was sitting with a bitch he told me he wasn't in a relationship with. His eye contact was strong though. So strong that I swear I was being pulled in his direction. But I didn't move. I matched the intensity of his stare, except I wore a frown on my face. I rolled my eyes and broke eye contact to say a few words to Jai.

"Where Jai go?" I asked Carla, who was busy giggling and talking with Pierre.

"I think she went to the restroom."

"Yeah, she went to the restroom Storm," said Ryan. "Everything aight, lil sis?"

Unlike my date, he noticed my frown off rip. Branden was busy taking his sixth shot, and scrolling through his phone.

228

"Yeah, I'm alright." I stood up and said, "Carla, walk with me boo."

She excused herself, and we headed for the restroom. I looked over my shoulder, over at Vice and his bitch. He was watching me. Like a child, I rolled my eyes really hard at him.

I intertwined my arm in Carla's and said, "Vice is here."

She whipped her head around so fast she smacked me in the face with her big hoop earrings, "What? Where he at? Girl, this is a sign from God! Go—"

I laughed, "A sign from God, Carla? He's with a female."

"Aw hell naw! Let's go over there. What the fuck!" Sometimes she could be wilder than Jai when it came to popping off.

"It's cool. As if you said, maybe it is a sign from God. A sign for me to stop thinking about his lying ass."

I was mad as fuck. I wanted to run over there and smack the piss out of him. Lying ass! Weak ass got me out here looking goofy as fuck. I mean, come on now Storm...you broke up with him. But fuck that!

He's so busy occupying his time with a broad he swore up and down he wasn't fucking with. They looked comfy as hell. Man...I can't even be this mad though. But my feelings are truly hurt.

I pushed the restroom door open, and almost fainted when I saw my best friend standing at the sink snorting a line of what I know for a fact was coke off her index finger.

"Jai...baby no!" I yelled.

She was off her ass though. She sat a small glass tube down, and placed her palms flat on the sink. Her head hung low, and she tilted her head to look up at me with glassy eyes.

"Here I come, sis. Give me a lil' minute," she replied, slurring over her words.

My heart was broken. Whatever the fuck I was just tripping over didn't matter anymore. My best friend...my sister...is on drugs. No...I can't have this shit.
"Carla...can you give us a minute?" I said with tears rolling down my face.

Carla looked over at Jai, and then back to me, "Yeah, hun." She gave me a hug, and walked out of the restroom.

I stood next to Jai at the sink and lifted her head by her chin, "Jai...baby...look at yourself."

She smacked my hand away, "Storm, gone somewhere. I'm cool sis. This is just something I do to take the edge off."

I grabbed her by her face and made her look in the mirror, "Bitch, look at you! You have powder on your nose, Jai! Look at yourself! Why are you doing this baby? Why!?"

She yanked her head away, wiped her nose, and said, "What you tripping about, damn!? It's only a little coke—"

"Only?! A little!?" I grabbed her purse and emptied it out on the counter. Five small glass tubes fell out, along with other things. What stood out the most was the fact that they all were empty.

I grabbed her shoulders and shook her as I talked, "Jai...please...please don't tell me you snorted all that shit in one day please."

She staggered a bit and tried to fight me away, "I'm grown, bitch. Grown. If I want to get high, I will!"

Jai was belligerent. Not only was she high off coke, but she had at least four shots of 1800. She kept trying to walk away from me, but she was staggering badly. She kept trying though and every time I grabbed her, she tried to fight me. Her eyes were bucked and she was hyper as hell. I was hurt. I'd never seen her act like this.

Finally, I was able to grab her in a hold too tight for her to break out of. Still, she kept trying to get loose. Her fighting caused us to hit the hard linoleum floor. I screeched out in pain, but I never let her go. I managed to pin her down between my legs. What the fuck was I supposed to do?

Jai went into a fit of laughter. I kept begging her to calm down, but she wouldn't.

"Chill bitch! You killing my high! Damn, now I'm gon' have to cop some more," she said, leaning back and yelling directly in my ear.

Someone tried to come into the restroom, but I quickly moved my leg from around Jai and kicked the door back closed.   .

"Come back later," I yelled.

"What?! Bitch I gotta pee," someone yelled back.

"And bitch you gon' wait," yelled Jai. "Don't call my best friend a bitch, ho!"

"What!?" The girl tried coming in again, and I kicked the door closed.

"Back the fuck up. Come back in fifteen minutes," I heard him say.

I rolled my eyes because despite it all, I was still highly pissed at him.

The girl walked away, I assumed, and in came Vice. He stood there with his hands stuffed in the pockets of his designer jeaned shorts, as usual. I looked up at him and rolled my eyes.

"What you rolling your eyes like a little girl for?" he asked with a smirk. "What's going on in here?"

Jai went to squirming again, and then came the laughter, "She killing my high, Vice! She tripping! I don't have shit else left. You got something on you? I know you told me you don't carry, but I need it!"

"Wait...hold on one mothafucking minute," I said with my eyes on him, "You knew about this?"

He shrugged and before he could get a word out of his mouth, Jai opened hers.

"Of course he knows, Storm. Who dope spot you think I cop from?"

I felt betrayed; even more than I did when I saw him sitting with what's-her-face. I was confused. I was hurt. Why would he allow this to happen?

"Nigga what?! You did this?!" I yelled as I stood to my feet, letting Jai go.

233

"I didn't do anything. She did that to herself, brown skin," said Vice, clearly unfazed by my anger. He still hadn't even took his hands out of his pockets. "Look, you gon' stand there and be mad at me, or do you want me to help get her ass out of here?"

"I'm straight. Go back to your date. I'm sure she's wondering where you are," I replied with my face scrunched up.

"What? Nigga you here with a bitch? You got my best friend fucked up," yelled Jai, holding onto the sink, trying to stand.

"Your friend broke up with me because she didn't want to disappoint dear old dad, so chill, aight?" he was talking to Jai, but looking at me. This was just too much. Too much drama. I hated to, but I cried. Not over him, but I was overwhelmed and had just witnessed my best friend snorting coke.

"What's wrong, Storm? This nigga hurting you? Vice, I'ma fuck you up," yelled Jai as she continued to struggle to stand.

"He can't hurt me. Fuck him," I said as I started to put Jai's things back in her purse.

"Fuck me? Those are harsh words coming from a little lady who still cares deeply for me," said Vice with a smile.

"Just leave us alone. Bye, we don't need your help. You've done enough!" I yelled, referring to him basically selling her drugs.

Vice turned away and touched the handle to the door, "It's only coke, brown skin, not crack. If you get her help now, she'll be straight."

I just waved him off, but he didn't leave out. He stood there staring at me; so hard that you would think he could see the soul of me. I avoided turning his way but after a while, I couldn't help but make eye contact with him. He was captivating. Enticing. Attracting. Alluring. I was drawn to him. Like a negative to a positive. Like a moth to a flame. I'm pissed, that's for certain, so why is my heart beating like this? Why are my hands becoming clammy? Why were there butterflies in the pit of my stomach?

He's so fucking handsome. He's breathtaking. Breathtaking and clearly seeing someone. I snatched my eyes away from his and helped Jai to her feet.

"I'm calling you later, so pick up," he ordered before leaving the restroom.

Finally, we were leaving the restroom after what felt like thirty minutes. Jai was doing a little better, but still high and drunk as hell. We had to go. Despite how people might feel, I had to get her out of there because if I didn't, she was definitely going to start some shit with the girl Vice was with. If not her, Jai was going to start some shit with someone. She was too crunk. Too turnt.

When we made it over to our section, Branden was standing. He was scowling at me. I was confused. Ryan met us halfway and took hold of Jai, who was having a hard time walking. I told him we had to go because she was too drunk. I wasn't about to tell him she was snorting. Jai said she didn't want to go home alone. I told her she wasn't; I was going home with her.

She laughed, "Sis, I love you but I want to go home with some dick, aight!?"

I laughed, and by then we were at our seats. Ryan agreed to safely get Jai home. I trusted him. So far, he's been nothing but a gentleman to her.

B still looked highly pissed. I didn't even bother asking him what was wrong, because I didn't give a fuck.

"Ay, I gotta go. Jai's too drunk," I said as I took my last puff from the hookah. "Carla, boo, you heard me?"

She was so busy giggling with Pierre that I really hated having to end their date. She didn't even say anything. Too busy caking it up.

"That ain't the reason you leaving, Storm, let's be real!" snapped B.

I looked at him like he'd lost his damn mind, "Boy, what?" I waved him off, "You drunk too. Sit down somewhere. Y'all killing the little buzz I did have!"

I wasn't confrontational when it came to men. Unlike Jai, if a man was hostile with me with their fists balled, I backed away. I wasn't going to fight a nigga. What the hell for? So I can get my ass whooped? Nah. If a nigga was tripping, I let him trip–and got the fuck out of dodge. Now, if he puts hands on me? I wouldn't hesitate to use my Taser on that ass.

"Nah, what I am is tired of being used," said Branden before puffing from the hookah. "That nigga play you and you come running back to me. Now you ready to jump back on his dick," he said, nodding in Vice's direction.

I quickly glanced over there, hoping he wasn't watching, but he was. Vice always watched me. Even while on a date. His date was watching too. Thing is, her face was screwed all up. She was pissed. I couldn't tell what Vice was.

I laughed, "B...I didn't go running back to shit. You approached me. You hit me up. The fuck?" I grabbed my clutch and said to Carla, "Boo. You gon stay here and finish your date or are you riding out with me?"

"Huh? What's going on," she asked, finally realizing that she and Pierre weren't the only people on Earth. Haha.

"Jai is drunk, but I'm guessing Ryan about to take her ho—"

"See, that's what the fuck I mean! You just said you were leaving because Jai drunk. Why you gotta leave if Ryan's taking care of her?" Branden took a shot, "You lying. You about to go fuck with that weak ass nigga," he said, staring across the room at Vice, who was smiling.
Lawd, I hope that nigga don't come over here acting an ass.

"Waaaait, what's wrong with this nigga," asked Carla as she stood to her feet. Pierre grabbed her by the waist and sat her down.

"Relax, beautiful," he said. "Cuz just in his feelings. You staying here with me, right?"

Carla looked up at me, and I shrugged.

"Awww shit, here comes that boss ass nigga Vice," said Jai while laughing.

I looked over my shoulder and met him half way before he could get to our section. I placed my palms on his chest and tried backing him up away from us. He grabbed my wrist and took my hands off his chest.

"Just go back to your date, Vice. Please."

I was blocking his path, and he kept trying to get around me, "Nah, it looks like my mans might have something to say to me. I'm just about to see what that is."

His date said, "And obviously he couldn't give a fuck less about his date. He too busy giving a fuck about basic bitches."

I looked past Vice, and at her, "Excuse me!?"

This time, Vice grabbed me and said, "Chill! I'll handle that later."

"No you chill! Don—"

Before I could finish my sentence, he quickly got around me and was standing in Branden's face. I headed in their direction, then turned around and said to his date, "Keep calm bitch. I can't be too basic, huh?"

Whatever she said after that was like 'whomp, whomp'. I wasn't hearing her. Whatever she said wasn't important. She wasn't throwing hands up, so she was irrelevant.

"Wassup, dog? You was saying something," said Vice with his hands behind his back, head turned to the side, leaning his ear toward B.

Branden took another shot. He was already doing too fucking much. He could barely stand, "I was saying...all this bitch give a fuck about is you!"

Vice cocked his head to the left and chuckled a little. When he unclasped his hands from around his back, I knew he was about to put them paws on Branden. That was an understatement though. He hit Branden so hard that he went flying on the table, knocking drinks and hookah down.

Everybody stood up. So much was going on. Both Ryan and Pierre were trying to get at Vice, but security was there before Branden could recover from the powerful blow.

Vice held his hands up, "Don't touch me. I'm leaving." He turned to me and said, "Stop fucking with niggas who don't respect the beauty of you." He walked away, and then turned and said, "Go home, lil mama."

An hour later, I was exactly where he told me to be. Not because I obeyed him, but because despite him being out with a bitch and supplying Jai with coke, I still wanted to talk to him. I didn't know how to feel. On one hand, I was extremely pissed at him, and on the other, I wanted nothing more than to feel the warmth of his mouth on mine. I missed him. I missed him so much that I was willing to risk losing my life and family by being with him.

I got out of the shower and grabbed my towel from the towel rack. I looked in a full-length mirror while I dried myself off. As the towel touched sensitive areas on my body, I thought of how long it'd been since I felt the feeling of a penis entering my love tunnel. So long. I yearned for it. I needed it badly.

As I was drying my hair with the towel, my phone rang. A bitch almost broke her neck running to the living room to answer it. I knew it was him, because my thirsty ass gave him a separate ringtone when I got in the house.

I snatched it off the charger and answered, "Hello."

"Open the door."

"Huh," I said out of confusion as I peeked out of the blinds.

There he stood. At my door, phone in hand, looking back at me.

"Hold on. I just got out of the shower," I said before rushing back to the bathroom to grab my robe.

As I was leaving the bathroom, I got a glimpse of myself in the mirror. On my chocolate skin was a few drops of water, my weave was wet and curly, and my face was, of course, bare. No filled in eyebrows, no lashes, not a bit of lipstick. I felt slightly self-conscious. I wanted to put on some lip gloss and eyeliner, but he eagerly knocked on the door.

"Fuck it," I mumbled as I headed back to the front door.

I unlocked it and before I could turn the doorknob to let him in, he did it for himself. The door swung open, and as soon as we lied eyes on each other, butterflies began to fill my stomach. Did I mention how attractive he was? God, I can't help but wonder if I've fallen in love?

Every time I'm around him, the hairs on the back of my neck stand. Every time he's near, I'm drawn to him. Like now, I want to grab hold of him. I want to kiss him. Hug him...touch him, but my pride wouldn't let me. So instead of embracing him, I stepped aside and he walked in. When he walked by, his hand grazed mine and I wanted to hold onto it. My heart rate sped, and I sighed as I closed the door behind him. Vice kicked his shoes off and took a seat on my couch.

"It smells nice in here," he said, looking over his shoulder at me. I was still standing by the door. Stuck.

"Yeah, thanks. It's the shower gel I use."

"You gon' sit down so we can talk?"

I nodded and walked over to the couch. Before I could sit down, he pulled me down onto his lap. Vice buried his face in my neck, inhaling.

"What are you doing?" I asked, giving little to no effort to pulling away from him.

"It smells even better on your skin," he said as he lifted his head and stared into my eyes. He bit his lips, and lowered his eyes to my lips. He wanted to kiss me, and I'd be lying if I said I didn't want to kiss him too. Vice, as bold as he always was, grabbed the back of my neck and planted the softest kiss upon my lips.

"Would you believe me if I told you that you've been on my mind like crazy?" he asked.

"No, I wouldn't," I shook my head. "I haven't heard from you in a month."

"The phone works both ways, brown skin." He smiled, "But there wasn't a day that your beautiful brown face didn't cross my mind."

I blushed, "Vice...I missed you so much."

He traced my lips with his finger, "I bet I missed you more."

I turned away at thoughts of him at the hookah bar with ol' girl earlier, "Nah, I'm sure you was pretty occupied."

He turned my head to face him, "Don't act like you weren't just out with that weak ass niggas. Stop playing, lil' mama."

CHAPTER TWENTY]
VICE

She was really sitting here trying to act like she wasn't entertaining whack niggas in my absence.

"Yeah well, okay," she replied with a shrug.

I pulled her into my chest, despite the water dripping from her hair. I wanted to feel her body against mine. I missed the fuck out of lil' mama, and I wasn't afraid to show her that. For the first time this week, a nigga felt right. That shit I was doing with Joslyn was only to occupy my mind and time, but as soon as I spotted Storm across the room at the hookah bar, it was like Joslyn never existed.

Real shit though. Joslyn was in my ear going on and on about how selfish I was, but I wasn't paying her any attention. She kept rapping about how she couldn't see what I saw in Storm – which was a fucking lie. Any person with two eyes could see that. Hell, even the blind could see the rarity and specialty of her. Whenever she walked in a room, her presence demanded attention. Joslyn saw that. She was just too much of a hater to give props where props were due.

Even without the makeup, false eyelashes, and lipstick, lil' mama was still the most beautiful woman I'd ever laid eyes on. The way her full lips curled up into a smile when she looked up at me with slanted brown eyes; she was beautiful, had a nigga in awe.

"What?" she asked as I stared down at her, speechless.

"Can a nigga sit back and take in the beauty of which overflows upon you?"

She laughed, "Nigga what? The beauty of which overflows upon me? You think you Shakespeare, huh?"

I laughed and playfully mushed her in the head, "Aight, yeah, you got me tripping on some poetic shit." I paused and held her tighter, "On some real shit though lil' mama, you got a nigga buggin."

"Hmmm, sounds to me like you're in love," she said with a smile.

I didn't respond. Instead, I grabbed the back of her neck and kissed her. Maybe shorty did have a point. Maybe I was in love, but I'd never come out and say that shit. She already had me out of my element. I wasn't about to allow her to think she had me wrapped around her finger, even if she did.

Storm stopped the kiss and said, "Vice...I can't let you go. I can't go another day without being with you." She shrugged, "Fuck it. I'm willing to piss a lot of people off to be with you." She paused, "If you'll have me?"

"Of course I'll have you," my eyes landed on the split in her robe exposing the ampleness of her breast, "All of you."

She smirked and said, "You can't have all of me yet."

I bit my lip and grabbed a hand full of her ass, "Don't tell me what I can't have, lil mama."

When a small moan escaped her mouth, I knew what was up. She wanted to give me the pussy. Storm straddled and wrapped her arms around me. My face rested in between her breast, and I inhaled. She smelled just as beautiful as she looked. Lil mama had me in my feelings, to the point where I really didn't give a fuck about the ringing of my phone. Whoever it was would just have to wait.

"Your phone..." she said as she lifted my head from her chest.

When our eyes met, I couldn't help but put my lips on hers.

She moaned and grabbed the back of my neck, intensifying the kiss. Her lips were so full, wet, and warm.

"Mmmh, wait, Vice it could be important," she said, interrupting the kiss.

I couldn't give a fuck less about what was on the other side of the phone. She was trying to stop the inevitable. She knew that if we went any further, she'd let me slid up in that pussy. That was my intention. A broad this pretty had to have some bomb ass pussy.

I bit my lip and said, "I bet your pussy taste as good as you look."

She shyly smiled and turned her head away, "Vice!"

I grabbed the tie on her robe and began to pull on it. She placed her hand on top of mine. I looked her in the eyes and said, "Why do that to yourself, brown skin?"

"Do...do what?"

"Deprive yourself of good dick."

Again, she shyly smiled and told me I had no filter.

"Let me do that for you," I said.

"Do what, Vice?"

I pulled her closer to me and whispered in her ear, "Make your toes curl, and body shiver."

"You talk a lot of shit."

I smiled and pulled the tie completely loose. The robe fell open, exposing her titties. Round, brown, and perky. Her nipples were standing at attention. She gasped and covered them. I grabbed her wrists and pulled her hands away. She let me. The whole time, my eyes didn't leave hers.

I ran my thumbs over her nipples, and she softly moaned. When she told me to stop, I knew she meant the exact opposite. I told her to make me stop, but she didn't. Instead, she arched her back, her nipples pointing right at me. I lowered my head and took them both in my mouth. Her titties were the perfect size...C cups maybe?

Storm grabbed the back of my neck, and pulled me in closer to her. She didn't want me to stop. She wanted the shit just as bad as me. I softly pulled on her nipples with my teeth, and she told me to bite them. I did, and softly ran my tongue along the roundness of her small areolas.

She was turned on, so badly that she was grinding on my dick through my pants. I snatched the robe completely off, and turned and laid her on the couch. She shyly covered her face.

"What you doing, girl?" I asked as I pulled her hands away.

"This ain't supposed to be happening."

I unbuckled my shorts and said, "Yes it is. If it wasn't destined to happen, then it wouldn't be."

I lowered my body on top of hers, and kissed her lips. Storm opened her legs, so that I could comfortably lie in between. My hands roamed her body, touching spots I've been wanting to touch since I first laid eyes on her beautiful ass.

"Ohhh, wait, wait, wait," she said as she squirmed.

I was easing my way up her inner thigh. The closer I got to her pussy, the heavier her breathing got. The closer I got to rubbing my fingers over her clitoris, the warmer it got between her legs.

She tried closing her legs. I wouldn't let her. I leaned closer to her ear and told her to stop fighting what she knew she wanted. Her eyes rolled into the back of her head, and her legs relaxed. I kissed and softly bit on her neck as I made my way up her thigh. Her legs began to tremble. I lifted my head from her neck and looked down at her face. She laid there with her eyes closed, eyebrows furrowed, and lips drawn into her mouth. So mothafuckin beautiful.

I told her she was beautiful simultaneously to my index finger brushing across her clit. She opened her eyes and stared into mine. Her mouth was slightly ajar. Her eyelashes fluttered as she rolled her eyes in the back of her head.

I lowered myself down her body. Her pussy felt puffy, and I wanted to see if it was just that. Nothing drove me crazier than a phat pussy, and when I finally laid my eyes on it, it was. Perfect, accompanied by a small button-sized clit. Freshly waxed, with the exception of a small patch sitting below her belly button. I parted her pussy lips with my fingers and slid my thumb inside. Wet, warm, and moist. The way her pussy held onto my finger made me wonder how it'd hug my dick.

I looked up at her, and she was in ecstasy. The look on her face told me so. She was biting down on her bottom lip, arms above her head holding onto the armrest of the couch. Eyebrows still wrinkled, eyes closed, with the sexiest frown ever on her face.

I removed my finger from her pussy, and it was covered in her thick creamy juices. I brought my hand up to my face and smelled my finger. Nothing. But still, it excited me and I sucked her juices off.

"Damn," I said.

She sat up and asked, "What's wrong?"

I stood up and said, "Nothing's wrong. Everything is just right, baby."

She eyed the imprint in my pants, and I told her to touch it. She sat on the edge of the couch and pulled my shorts down. When they hit the floor, she stared at my dick peeking through the hole of my boxers.

"Pull it out, Storm," I told her. She seemed scared. Unmoving. So I grabbed her hand and placed it on my dick. She gasped and mumbled how she'd never had anything so big.

[CHAPTER TWENTY ONE]
STORM

His dick was big. Too big, if that makes any sense? I was scared of that mothafucka. When I finally mustered up enough courage to pull his boxers down, I backed up a little. He looked to be about ten inches. It was so thick though, maybe by two and a half inches, and covered in thick, protruding veins. The head of his dick was in a perfect mushroom shape. What surprised me probably more than the size of his dick was the fact that his pubic hair was neatly trimmed.

"Vice..."

He held his dick in his hands, "What? You scared of it, baby?"

I shook my head, "I just haven't had anything that big before. I mean, I've only had sex with three guys. That shit is going to bust me way o—"

He placed his index finger over my lips and said, "Chill. I'm not going to hurt you. Lay back down."

He was so bossy, and I loved it. I laid back down, and he kicked his boxers away. When he lifted his shirt over his head, I couldn't help but think 'damn'. He was ripped. Tattoo's covered almost every inch of his upper body.

Vice laid in between my legs, and then bent my knees. He made a trail of kisses from my lips down to my belly button, where he lingered for a bit. He was teasing me. He went lower, and softly flicked his tongue over my clit before kissing my thighs. He moved further north, kissing my legs, and then each and every one of my toes.

Vice made his way back up. He went from kissing behind my knees, directly to putting his mouth on my pussy. He softly suckled on my clitoris, while making circles in my pussy with his index finger. I grabbed the back of his head, begging for more of his tongue. He was teasing me, still. Softly licking, and flicking his tongue on it.

"Please," I begged.

"Please?" he asked before lightly blowing on it.

"Yessss."

He then replaced his finger with his tongue. I was taken by surprised at how skillfully he moved his tongue in and out of me, with his thumb going to work on my clit. I couldn't control the fit of tremors my body went into. I felt myself backing away from his brutal, but pleasurable tongue fucking.

He grabbed hold of my waist, pulling me back down to him, "Don't run from what you begged for."

He held me so tight that I could barely move.

"Nooo, I'm about to cum. Waaait," I said, steady trying to get away from him.

And then he stopped. With no warning, he removed his hands from my waist, and his tongue from my vagina. I opened my eyes and watched as he retrieved a Magnum XL condom from his shorts pocket.

He tore it open, and I stopped him before he could slide it on.

"No...let me," I said, grabbing the condom from him.

Vice stood up, and his dick stood at attention, in my face. I grabbed hold of it, and rubbed the pre-cum oozing from his penis onto the head of his dick. He closed his eyes and tilted his head back. I rubbed his dick on my face, and softly smacked it on my cheek. His dick was so heavy. Made me wonder how thick his cum would be when he finally did orgasm.

I wrapped my lips around the head of his dick and softly sucked. He made a noise that told me he was enjoying this. I licked the sides of his dick and eased it down my throat, trying my best not to gag, but I did and when it happened, slob dripped from my mouth. I looked up at him, shocked at him looking right at me. Our eyes stayed on each other's as I continued to suck on him. I took his dick from my mouth and rubbed it all over my face again, watching as he bit on his bottom lip, and his eyes rolled to the back of his head.

Finally, I slid the condom over his dick. I bent over on the couch, anticipating how uncomfortable him entering me was about to be, but what happened next surprised me.

He roughly turned me over and laid me back down on the couch, in missionary position. He pinned my legs over my head.

"Don't move," he ordered.

I nodded and chewed on the inside of my cheeks.

He slowly entered me, and I felt my walls being stretched open. I closed my eyes, "Ssssssshit."

"Open your eyes, Storm," said Vice as he continued to enter me, slowly, inch by inch.

I opened my eyes, and stared into the fire in his eyes.

"Oh God," I managed to say when he was finally inside of me.
He looked down at his dick, moving in and out of me.

"Don't. Move," he said again as he let my legs go.

257

Vice lowered his head and bitch...oh my mothafucking...he licked my clit–while his dick was still inside of me. I threw my head back and let out a moan so loud, I swear it came from the pit of my soul.

"Mmmmh, shit, Vice what are...you doing to meeeee?"

He didn't say anything. He continued to flick his tongue on my clit as he increased the moving of his hips. He was fucking and giving me head at the same time. I've never felt anything like it. I was in orgasmic heaven. I couldn't even close my mouth.

He kissed my clit before stopping, and holding onto my hips. He took his dick out and slapped it on my clit before entering me whole. I squirmed and tried to get away from him. This was too much. His dick...was too big. I could feel him in the center of my stomach.

Vice pinned my legs back again, and fucked me in a slow, deep rhythm.

"Why you keep trying to run from this dick, huh lil' mama?" he asked as he poked at a sensitive spot.

I couldn't respond. Hell, a bitch was lost for words.

My eyes rolled to the back of my head as I felt an orgasm coming on. I threw my head back again and moaned his name as I came all over his dick. Vice removed his dick and replaced it with his tongue. He dipped his tongue in my pussy, devouring my cum. He put his dick back inside of me and lowered his mouth onto mines. I tasted sweet.

"Bend over," he said.

I bent over and he grabbed hold of my ass cheeks, spreading them open as he gave me deep, long strokes.

"Damn..." he mumbled.

I was starting to adjust to the size of him. I looked over my shoulder and came at the look on his face. On his face was a look of pure enjoyment. Vice's eyebrows were wrinkled, his top teeth were over his bottom lip, and there were small sweat beads on his forehead. He held onto me, slowly pulling out only leaving the tip in.

I threw my ass back, and my pussy made a gushy noise causing both of us to say "shit."

Vice put my leg over the back of the couch and increased the speed of his fucking. He slammed his dick in and out of me, and I enjoyed it.

"Damn lil' mama," he said as he heavily panted.

I felt his dick pulsating, and knew he was getting ready to cum. When I heard his breathing switch up, I hurried up and pulled away from his dick. Before he could react, I was on my knees with his dick in my hands, pulling his condom off just in time for him to bust on my face.

Vice brought out the whole freak in me.

Life was great. If that means basically not having parents or a best friend, then yeah, life was fucking great. The only thing that made it great was the fact that Vice has constantly been in my life, despite the fact that I got into a big argument with my parents the other day. I let them know that I was seeing him regardless of the ill feelings they had towards him.

Mack – my daddy – almost made me slip up and tell my momma about his old ass being back in the drug game. I swear, I came close, but the look he gave me when I started to hint at it sent chills down my spine. I should've! What more could he do to me? He cut me off completely, and I've always been dependent of him. Not because I had to, but because that's just what I was accustomed to. He took my car and said he wasn't paying the rent at my crib anymore. I wouldn't give a fuck if the rent wasn't over a thousand dollars a month. I should've known better than to accept a house I couldn't afford on my own. A year ago, when he rented it for me, I didn't know I'd end up dealing with someone that would eventually cause him to cut me off.

Vice is taking care of everything though. That'd be great if I actually wanted him to. I felt like a burden to him. He copped me a 2015 Dodge Charger, and he paid my rent up for a year. He insisted on moving me up out of the crib, but I declined. I would've declined the car offer too, if it wasn't for me having to go back and forth to work. Speaking of work, the nigga wanted me to quit. Things were moving way too fast. Life was moving far too quickly. In a week's span, all of this had happened.

Did you notice how I said I didn't have a best friend a minute ago? Well, I didn't mean that literally. Jai and I ain't beefing or anything like that, but she's been avoiding me. She won't even talk to me. Every time I hit her up, she has an excuse to hang up – that's if she even answers the phone. Most of the time, she just shoots me a text. We've never had this problem before, and that's because before recently, Jai's never done coke. That's the only reason she was avoiding me. My boo was embarrassed, and I was trying my hardest to let her know she didn't have to be.

I was chilling on my patio sipping from a glass of Moscato, trying to figure out how I was going to get Jai to talk to me for more than five minutes. I missed her so much. More than anything, I wanted to get her help. According to Vice, she'd still been coping. I'm pissed the fuck off about him being her dealer. I told him to stop selling to her. He told my ass no. Vice reminded me that him not selling to her wasn't going to stop her from snorting. Cold honesty for my ass.

"What's on your mind, lil mama?" asked Vice, sliding my patio doors back closed.

"Jai. I'm going to The Crazy Horse tonight."

He sipped from my glass and nodded, "Aight, bet. I'm rolling through there with you. Niggas be on some animal shit up there at that time."

"Okay. What time is it?"

He looked down at his designer watch, "Almost ten." He frowned, "Why you drinking this weak shit? Ay, I'ma meet you there. I got some shit to take care of, beautiful."

I rolled my eyes and took my glass from him, "Because I like it, punk. Alright, I'm heading that way at eleven."

I told him alright like I didn't care about him leaving, but I did. He was always busy with something. The streets were talking, and although I didn't live in the hood, I knew what was up. Thanks to Facebook, I knew of all the beef going on over on Seven Mile and Riopelle.

What scared me was the fact that the problems he was having weren't only with my daddy. I knew he wasn't the most liked person in the hood, but whoever these niggas were, they were straight up gunning for Vice. In addition to dealing with beef, he was getting heat from the police. I knew fucking with a drug dealer was stressful, but I didn't know the stress would start this damn soon.

Vice kissed me on the forehead and lips before leaving.

I sighed and slipped my flip-flops on to head back in the house. I wasn't dressed. All I had on was my robe. Vice and I had just fucked in the shower and when I got out, I didn't bother putting on clothes because I didn't have plans on going anywhere. I missed my best friend though, and was going to force her ass to speak to me.

I decided to wear a simple pair of sky blue Nike yoga pants, and a fitted black t-shirt. On my feet were a pair of Nike running shoes. I wore my hair in a low ponytail. I was on some laidback chill shit. I wasn't going to the club to party, so I didn't care to dress up.

My phone notification went off, and I checked it.

Carla (10:41PM): U talk 2 her?

Me (10:41PM): Nope. OMW to The Crazy Horse.

Carla (10:42PM): Come scoop me.

Me (10:42PM): Alright. Pulling up in 5.

Twenty minutes later, Vice and I were pulling up at The Crazy Horse at the same time. When he got out of the car, I saw anger written all over his face, even if he did try to mask it with a smile. When he pulled me in for a hug, I asked him what was wrong. He just smiled and told me shit was sweet. I knew he was lying. Vice introduced me to the guy he was with, as his cousin Dawson. He was visibly pissed, too.

I introduced Carla to them, and it was obvious that Dawson had taken a liking to her. Vice grabbed my hand as we walked into the club.

Gone shake that ass bitch, I'ma throw this money
Gone shake that ass bitch, I'ma throw this money
Gone shake that ass bitch I'ma throw this money
I'ma throw this money, I'ma throw this money.

The popular 2007 USDA hit Throw this Money was blasting from the club's speakers. On the stage was a bad ass red bone, bent over making her phat ass clap. She was killing it, and the customers were loving it. One guy was emptying a duffle bag full of money on her. Damn, I wondered if sis was getting it like that.

"What time do she go on," yelled Carla in my ear.

"I don't know. I'm about to find out," I yelled back.

Your man on the road, he doin' promo
You said, "Keep our business on the low-low"

I'm just tryna get you out the friend zone
Cause you look even better than the photos
I can't find your house, send me the info
Drivin' through the gated residential
Found out I was comin', sent your friends home
Keep on tryna hide it but your friends know

The music switched to The Weekend – The Hills, and the dancer on the stage climbed the pole to the ceiling, and seductively slid down. The way she moved reminded me of that popular stripper, Mizhani.

Vice and his boys walked in front of us. I'd occasionally peep how Dawson would lean over, say something in Vice's ear, and point to the back of the club. Even the workers in the club were whispering to each other. Every time we passed one of them, they'd whisper to their coworker. I didn't know what the fuck the talk was about. Let me check Facebook...I know somebody saying something.

I went in my bag and pulled my phone out. Before I could open my Facebook app, Carla bumped me on the shoulder to grab my attention. She pointed to the DJ booth, where we could find out what time Jai was scheduled to go on. I put my phone back in my purse and caught up with Vice and them.

"Yeah, Oozy. You remember dude?" I heard Dawson ask Vice.

Vice rubbed his chin, "Yeah, big nigga that ran with Hustle Hard…"

I interrupted them and told Vice I was about to go to the DJ booth to ask about Jai. He nodded and told me he was right behind me.

Carla and I made our way through the thick crowds and approached the DJ booth.

"Hey. What time is Barbie hitting the stage?" I yelled at him.

He bobbed his head to the music and said, "Next. Genie about to hop off."

I thanked him and left the booth.

We stood back, vibing to the music. When Genie finally left the stage, I told Carla Jai was up next. The DJ called her name over the mic, but she didn't come out. He called her a few more times, and I started to get worried. I went back up to the booth and asked him what was going on. He told me he didn't know, and then he called another dancer.

"What's wrong, brown skin?" asked Vice, noticing the frown on my face.

"Jai didn't hit the stage. I need to find her," I said.

"Aight, hold up. She fuck with Genie tough. I'ma find out what's going on. Don't worry bout it, lil' mama."

He knew I'd been bugging out about Jai's wellbeing since I caught her snorting. The club was slapping, which is why I couldn't understand why she hadn't hit the stage. There was serious bread to be made, and Jai loved everything associated with making money.

"I wonder what's going on," said Carla as Vice walked in the direction of the dressing room.

Someone was near the bar causing a lot of commotion. We turned our attention over there just as the DJ cut the music.

"Ay, ay, ay! What the fuck's going on ov—"

"Somebody about to jump off the fuckin roof!" yelled some guy.

As soon as the words left his mouth, everybody went running for the exit. So many people were rushing out that the shit was like a stampede. Dawson grabbed hold of Carla and me so we wouldn't be knocked to the floor. I looked over my shoulder, trying to find Vice. As expected, he was running my way.

He grabbed hold of me, and we made our way out of the club.

"It's Barbie! What the fuck she doing up there?"

My heart dropped at the mention of Jai's stage name. Vice held me tighter.

Carla yelled, "Oh my fucking God!"

She and Dawson had made it out before us. Seeing her with her hand clasped over her mouth scared me. When we finally got outside, I looked up and there my best friend was, cup in her hand, swaying left and right.

"Y'all came to see Barbie huh," she yelled as she staggered towards the edge of the building.

"Jai...baby, please," I managed to shout over the voices of everyone else.

"Storm, bitch you came to see me too huh?" she yelled before bursting out laughing.

"Baby, please get off that ro—"

BLOCKA, BLOCKA, BOOM, BOOM, BOOM!

Shots rang out and I fell to the ground, trying to keep my eyes on Jai. I couldn't see her though. People were running, some tripping over me. I tried to stand up, but Vice pushed me back down.

"Brown skin! Stay down," he yelled as he went for the gun on his waist as shots continued to be fired.

"Is Jai o—"

Before I could ask about Jai someone had answered my question for me, "Oh my God, she's falling"

To be continued...

Us Against Everybody: Miss Candice

Join our mailing list to get a notification when Leo
Sullivan Presents has another release!
Text LEOSULLIVAN to 22828
to join!
Last release:
Lady Bang 2: A Knockout Story
Check out our new and upcoming releases on the
next page! Click the new releases image below to read for
FREE with Kindle Unlimited
To submit a manuscript for our review, email us at
leosullivanpresents@gmail.com
*Join our mailing list to get a notification for these
upcoming releases!*

Us Against Everybody: Miss Candice

CPSIA information can be obtained
at www.ICGtesting.com
Printed in the USA
LVOW04s1738021216
515533LV00009B/578/P